# Orphaned and Alone?

"Cousin Tirzah. . ." I say softly, thinking maybe now we can understand each other. Maybe now I can argue her out of selling me and Pheme.

I am mistaken.

"I warned you this would happen. You wouldn't listen," Cousin Tirzah says, and briskly pushes back her chair. She stands up and looks at me coolly. I can see her mind is made up. "Mr. Pug Ryan is a patient, God-fearing man, but he won't bide his time forever. A deal is a deal. I'm letting him know tomorrow that he can take you and your brother off my hands, once and for all."

"But Cousin Tirzah, what happens if Pa gets here and we're gone?" I ask, my voice rising with panic.

"It's God's will," she whispers, her hot breath rushing past my cheek. "I've waited long enough. Your pa isn't ever coming back."

**Books by Laurie Lawlor**

The Worm Club
How to Survive Third Grade
Addie Across the Prairie
Addie's Long Summer
Addie's Dakota Winter
George on His Own
Gold in the Hills

*Heartland series*

Come Away with Me
Take to the Sky
Luck Follows Me

Available from MINSTREL Books

# Gold
## in the Hills

## Laurie Lawlor

A
MINSTREL®
BOOK

Published by POCKET BOOKS
New York   London   Toronto   Sydney   Tokyo   Singapore

A Minstrel Book published by
POCKET BOOKS, a division of Simon & Schuster Inc.
1230 Avenue of the Americas, New York, NY 10020

Copyright © 1995 by Laurie Lawlor

Published by arrangement with Walker and Company

ISBN: 0-671-56833-7

First Minstrel Books printing May 1997

10  9  8  7  6  5  4  3  2  1

A MINSTREL BOOK and colophon are registered trademarks of Simon & Schuster Inc.

Cover art by Diane Sivavec

Printed in the U.S.A.

Gold
in the Hills

# ONE

Old Judge's log cabin crouches beside Lone Squaw Lake, half hidden by jack pines and boulders. The yard's heaped with cast-off tin cans, broken crates, fish bones, and rusted wagon wheels. Smoke pours from the chimney. I've heard about the man who lives here—the most despicable, cantankerous hermit this side of the Continental Divide. Even so, my twelve-year-old brother and I intend to slip past. Crossing Old Judge's place is the fastest way back to the footbridge that leads to Cousin Tirzah's. And we don't have a moment to lose.

I grab Pheme's arm before he can bolt across the yard. "What if he catches us?" I whisper.

Pheme jabs me hard with his elbow. For once, I shut up. But all I can think about is what's going to happen to us. He dashes for the footbridge. I take a deep breath and follow, leaping over a heap of crates. Next time I look, he's crossed the inlet and disappeared into the woods on the other side.

Now it's my turn.

The bridge is only two logs wide, suspended across a pile of rocks in the middle of the river. There's no handrail. I won't look down. I won't think about how I can't swim. The old logs sag and creak under my weight. If a rotten part gives way, I'll tumble into the swirling water and drown for sure. Mustn't think about falling. Mustn't think about drowning. Slowly, I inch my way across. I pray that Cousin Tirzah will forgive us for breaking the Sabbath and going into town to check for a letter from Pa. Dear God, if I make it across I promise I—

My prayers are interrupted by wild, ferocious barking. Waiting on the other side is the ugliest, meanest-looking half-mongrel, half-coyote I have ever seen. The dog bares his sharp teeth and stares at me with yellow eyes steady as a snake's. His tattered ears lie flat against his narrow, evil head. The mangy brown fur on his back bristles straight up, and I can hear a low warning rumble coming from deep inside his chest.

I drop to my hands and knees and hold tight to the footbridge, too terrified to go forward or retreat. The river hisses and sprays my face. "Go home, dog! Pheme! Help!"

No answer.

Desperately, I heave a piece of limp bark from the foot-bridge log. The dog prowls closer and crouches, ready to pounce. "Help me! Somebody help me!" I scream.

"Let her be!" a loud voice booms.

The dog retreats to the edge of the woods, tail between his legs. I crawl off the bridge onto solid land and stumble gratefully to my feet. Who rescued me? The underbrush shakes and out steps none other than Old Judge. He's short and wiry and he's got a long, mean-looking rifle under one arm. His stained, battered hat is pulled down over his forehead so far that I can see only his too-long nose and square chin. A drooping, grizzled mustache hides his mouth. "You know you're trespassing?" he says gruffly.

"Yes, sir." My knees wobble like a newborn calf's. I've heard Old Judge raises yellow cats for their hides. I reckon anybody who does anything that awful isn't naturally a forgiving kind of person. What if he skins intruders, too?

"This is *my* private property. Nobody comes around here asking me for help. Can't say I remember the last time anybody asked me for anything. You have a loud scream, you know it?"

I nod, too flustered to speak. I glance around for a sign of yellow cats. I don't see any. Maybe every last one's dead and scalped.

"Well, I helped you. Now get."

I gulp and try to feel brave. All Old Judge did for me was to call off his dog and he's acting like he just jumped in the river and got himself all wet saving me from drowning. I coax my legs but they won't move. The dog snarls. I wonder if it's safe to turn my back on the mongrel and walk away.

"Thought I told you to leave," Old Judge says, and scowls. "My dog Sinbad isn't going to hurt you. But I just might. Do you know who I am?"

"Yes, sir." I keep my eye on that long gun and try to think of the most flattering thing I can say. "You have a famous reputation, sir."

"Humph! Are we having a conversation here? I don't remember starting this little discussion. I don't ordinarily waste my time talking to people, especially people who trespass on my private property."

"Sorry, sir."

"You should be sorry, sorry as a sinner. In fact, that's a good name for you. Sinner."

Now it's my turn to feel insulted. "My name is not Sinner. My name is Harriet Elizabeth Proctor."

"You mean you're not one of Tirzah Throckmorton's mongrels?"

"I am *not*," I say, indignant that anyone should think me a direct blood relation to Cousin Tirzah's children. "Like I said, my name is Harriet Elizabeth Proctor. I am from Springfield, Illinois. I'm ten years old. And I have a brother, Pheme. His real name is Alexander Phimester Proctor. And our father is rich and famous and we're just staying with Cousin Tirzah and the Throckmorton family for the summer while he prospects for gold."

"That the truth, is it, Sinner?" He doesn't look as if he believes a word I said.

"My name is not Sinner, sir," I say slowly, controlling my temper as much as I can because I can tell Old Judge is enjoying making me mad.

"How come you're not afraid to talk to me, like everyone else?"

"Should I be, sir?" I reply, sweet and innocent as I can.

"Your brother certainly is." Old Judge waves toward the trees. "Come on over here!"

Sheepishly, Pheme appears from between a grove of aspens. As he walks closer, he kicks rocks and keeps his mouth shut. The first thing you notice about Pheme is his eyes. He has big, moody dark eyes that stick out. My brother sees everything with those eyes. I swear he can look directly inside people and tell what they're thinking. He knows right away when he meets strangers if they're going to make fun of him for the way he stutters. Since we've come to Colorado, he's hardly said one word aloud.

As soon as Pheme stands beside me, Old Judge announces, " 'Unbidden guests are often welcomest when they are gone.' *Richard the Third,* Act Two."

Pheme looks over the old man carefully. My brother's short and skinny for his age, with the same freckles I have. His hair is deep brown and straight as broom bristles instead of unruly, black, and wiry, like mine. Pheme twists his fingers the way he does when he's concentrating. He has the finest, palest hands, just like Pa's. He checks his back pocket for his sketchbook. Then he whispers something in my ear.

I clear my throat. Now it's my turn to feel pleased. "Excuse me, sir. But my brother says you're wrong."

"I'm what?"

Pheme prods me with his elbow. I clear my throat nervously. "My brother says for me to tell you," I continue, "it's not *Richard the Third.* It's *Henry the Sixth.*" I hold my breath, expecting at any moment to be blown to bits.

Old Judge levels his gaze directly at Pheme. "*King Henry* it is. You're absolutely correct. I can tell that you have a masterful command of the plays of the great bard, William Shakespeare—a very rare skill in these parts. Therefore, I will call you Boss." Old Judge puts one finger to the brim of his hat as if he's making some kind of salute.

Pheme blushes.

"And I have one word of advice for you both. Don't you or Sinner here ever come uninvited on my property again. You understand?"

Pheme nods, grabs my hand, and sets off at a gallop. Old Judge's laughter echoes across the lake as we disappear deeper into the forest, out of range of his rifle.

The next day Cousin Tirzah's guest cabin is empty. An empty guest cabin puts Cousin Tirzah in a raw mood. She frets that she won't have another paying guest the rest of the summer. We don't pay much attention to her complaints. After all, no guests means fewer chores for us.

Cousin Tirzah owns two cabins about a hundred yards from Lone Squaw Lake. The biggest is for her boarders, who come to hunt and trap. There are eight beds and cots in the guest cabin, which is divided with muslin sheets hung from ropes to make three bedrooms. Each has its own wooden crate turned on end to serve as a stand for a basin, a pitcher, and a chunk of homemade lye soap in an empty sardine can. On the floor beside each bed is a rag rug Cousin Tirzah made. She is proud of her guest cabin. "It isn't fancy, but it's clean," she reminds guests, who are forbidden to spit tobacco juice on the floor, use liquor, or smoke in bed.

Pheme and I and Cousin Tirzah and her four children live in the other cabin, which has just two rooms: one for eating, one for sleeping. Since the three available beds are already filled, Pheme and I sleep on the kitchen floor. In the morning when it's still cold and dark, Pheme and I have to get up quickly and stow away our bedding.

Mist on Lone Squaw Lake doesn't burn off until the sun

has been up for an hour or more. Gloomy mountain walls and forests make me feel trapped and choked for breath. Back home, there were no enormous mountains or trees to block my view. The prairie stretched for miles, and I could watch the weather come in and see the sun rise and fall behind the perfectly flat horizon. In this steep valley, I can't see a storm until it's overhead. I get lost and can't tell which way is east or west. Living here is like living in the bottom of a deep mine shaft, never once being able to see out.

Steep mountain walls don't seem to bother Cousin Tirzah. Every morning she comes in the kitchen and sets up the table, two long planks balanced on sawhorses and covered with a worn oilcloth. Then she thanks God for the place we live and the food we eat and hands us our morning meal of boiled cornmeal or maybe pearled rice and milk. A big noon meal for us might be a bowl of antelope soup with some wet dough put in, plus fried onions, a piece of bread with butter and syrup, and a spoonful of dried apples. For supper we usually have mush, same as breakfast. The food is plain-tasting and there's not much of it. My stomach hasn't stopped growling since we came.

When we finish breakfast, Cousin Tirzah hands us brooms to sweep the floor and set out dishes of flapjacks, fried pork, and potatoes—and plenty of hot coffee—for the guests. After we wash breakfast dishes, we go out in the little garden beside the cabin to pick bugs off the melon vines and the potato plants. It's important to go out early when the bugs are stupid. Cousin Tirzah showed us how to search every hill and catch the bugs and pinch their heads off so they won't riddle the leaves.

There isn't anything I hate as much as housework, and

from dawn till dusk, that is all I ever seem to do. The fact that Cousin Tirzah's lazy thirteen-year-old daughter, Patience, and I have to work together is unfortunate, since we can hardly tolerate the sight of each other. Every day we make all the beds. We gather eggs, beat rugs, and delouse the mattresses until I'm about worn out. We work so dreadful hard.

Whenever Patience gets a chance, she preaches to me on Judgment. She thinks she knows everything about how to get into the Kingdom of Heaven. She says I've got the wrong religion since I'm not Methodist. She says I'm not willing to humble my heart before Jesus and I don't follow the path of the Righteous. If she weren't so much bigger than me, I'd show Miss High and Mighty a thing or two.

This morning, we finished chores early. Baby Willie, just two years old, sits in an empty bushel basket and watches Pheme and me play "Horse Thieves and Vigilantes" with Patience, six-year-old Minnie, and their brother, eleven-year-old Eddie. Eddie invented the game so he has an excuse to make people cry.

"Line up!" Eddie orders in his usual bossy fashion. "Line up! You, too, dogie," he says to my brother, as if he's nothing but a weak motherless calf. I give Eddie a hard look like I'm going to knock him flat, but he doesn't pay any attention to me. Instead he trots on an invisible horse around trampled space between the cabins. He gives rocks to Patience and Minnie. Only Vigilantes get to chuck rocks.

Pheme and I are Horse Thieves. We're outnumbered and hiding in an abandoned mine shaft, which is really a group of boulders behind the guest cabin. Our weapons are just willow branches.

"This is the law!" Eddie yells. "Come out with your hands up."

"Never!" I shout bravely.

"That's not what you're supposed to say. You're supposed to give up so we can shoot you and hang you proper," Eddie announces. "We're going to kill you just the same as they did last year in Lulu City."

"Tell it again, Eddie," Minnie says eagerly, hugging her skinny arms.

I put my hands over my ears whenever Eddie tells about miners blown to bits by dynamite, crushed by collapsed shoring, or smashed by runaway ore wagons. Since this isn't a dead-miner story, I listen.

"Last year in Lulu City," Eddie says, "six of the vilest cutthroats who ever lived were shot to pieces by an armed posse. The bodies were dragged into town and put on display."

"Everybody went," Minnie chimes in. "It was real entertaining."

"Children!" Cousin Tirzah interrupts from the cabin doorway. "Stop playing and come here at once."

"Oh, Ma! Not now!" Eddie whines. "We were just getting to the good part."

Cousin Tirzah shakes her finger. "There are chores to be done, Edward. Mr. Cairns from town just told me that real English royalty—a Lord Somebody-or-Other—is coming up over Berthoud Pass with four servants and a half-dozen horses and burros. He plans to stay here and do some hunting, and I need firewood chopped and laundry washed. No back talk or I get out the strap, you understand?"

"Yes, ma'am," Eddie mumbles.

Cousin Tirzah orders Pheme to haul water from the lake. Patience and Minnie are to build a fire in the yard to heat water for laundry. "Harriet Elizabeth Proctor," Cousin Tirzah barks, "you bring Willie inside. I have something to say to you in private."

Patience gives me a High and Mighty smile because she knows I'm in trouble again.

# TWO

W hat is it, ma'am?" I ask. With Willie on one hip, I linger in the doorway and hope for a quick escape. No luck.

"Come in here," says Cousin Tirzah, who does not even look up. She sits at the table and studies numbers in her ledger book. She licks the end of a pencil stub and makes one of her hen scratch marks, frowns, and rubs her wrinkled forehead.

Cousin Tirzah's gray eyes are deep-set and sorrowful. She is not a tall woman, but her arms and broad back are amazingly powerful. I've seen her hoist a sixty-five-pound bag of salt as if it were only goose down. One moonless night she took after a prowling coyote with only a piece of fence railing. She is proud of her fearlessness the way another woman might be proud of her fine quilt stitching.

Everything about Cousin Tirzah is thick and sturdy and tidy. She is never without her spotless flour sack sunbonnet.

When she moves, it is like the force of God. Not for one moment is she idle. She despises everything but work, work, work.

I have never once heard Cousin Tirzah laugh or seen her smile. Maybe that's because she's had too much hard luck or because she lives too close to the sky or because her husband, Mr. Throckmorton, up and left her here with all the children. I don't know. With the exception of Willie, I can't say I've ever seen any of Cousin Tirzah's children kiss her or tell her something tender. When I used to kiss Mama's cheek, her skin felt soft and fine as a peach. Maybe no one kisses Cousin Tirzah because her skin is so leathery and tough. Besides, it's hard to kiss a person who never laughs or smiles.

"Girl," Cousin Tirzah says, "take a look at these sums."

I place Willie on the floor and sit at the table. Is this some kind of a schoolteacher trick? If she wanted to have somebody add, she should have asked Pheme. Of course, nobody around here believes Pheme has a brain. So she's making her point with me. I stare in confusion at the column of numbers. Arithmetic is my worst subject, after spelling.

"Sixty-three. You see that? That's how many days I have left this season for paying guests to stay in my guest cabin. I have to fill that cabin every night to make thirty-nine dollars and ninety-five cents' profit—that's after I subtract for my costs of feeding the guests."

"Thirty-nine dollars and ninety-five cents?" I ask, bewildered.

"Snow comes in October some years—maybe sooner. Nobody comes over the pass. My guest cabin is empty. That thirty-nine dollars and ninety-five cents plus what I take in for doing laundry is all I have for flour and beans and rice to feed five people. If your pa doesn't come back," Cousin Tirzah continues, shooting me an accusing glance, "that will make seven people. Seven people living on thirty-nine dollars and ninety-five cents means a mighty hungry winter. Don't go deaf, girl. You understand me?"

I gulp. "Pa will come back. He promised. I expect a letter any day."

"Well, I hope for your sake you're right. Gold fever has a cursed way of making a man lose track of everything, including time," Cousin Tirzah snarls. She turns the ledger book page and points to a row of penciled check marks. "You and your brother are a burden to me. You've been taking food out of my children's mouths for thirty-six days—ever since you came."

"Pa will pay you, soon as he comes." I try to smile, even though my stomach churns. Thirty-six days. "Ma'am, may I go now?"

"No, not until you hear me out. Girl, either you and your brother leave by winter or I must find some way to get more money. Do I make myself clear?"

I nod weakly.

"Before you go help Patience with the laundry, I have one more thing to say."

"Yes, ma'am?"

"Don't try my goodwill. You're sinful and disobedient. You and your halfwit brother ran away from Sabbath yesterday. Don't ever do that again." Cousin Tirzah slams shut her ledger book. "The wrath of God is like a rod of iron."

"Yes, ma'am," I say, feeling as if somebody just knocked

the wind out of me. I run outside. A letter. If only Pa would send us word when he's coming. Then I could prove to Cousin Tirzah that he hasn't forgotten about me and Pheme. Pa will return. He promised. But try as I may, I can't stop Cousin Tirzah's threat from ringing in my ears.

"Hattie, help me lift the kettle," Patience shouts to me.

I take one side of the sloshing iron kettle, and together we hook the handle to a bar over the fire. I hate doing laundry.

As soon as the water boils, we set the rinse tub where smoke won't blow in our eyes, since the wind is pert. We sort one pile white, one pile colored, one pile work britches and rags. Patience dumps lye-soap shavings into the boiling water. I rub the dirty spots against the scrub board till my fingers hurt. With a broomstick handle, Patience lifts white sheets out of the boiling kettle and dips them in the rinse tub.

Cousin Tirzah likes things clean. She likes things persnickety neat. The moment she saw me, I suppose she decided I'd be shiftless and disappointing.

The day we first met Cousin Tirzah she was standing at her cabin door. She didn't smile or say hello. "Kind of scrawny, aren't they?" she said, looking through me and Pheme as if we were panes of dirty glass. "Hope they don't got the cough, too."

"They're healthy and good workers and they'll be here only until fall, when I return," Pa replied. He tried with all his handsome charm to coax a grin out of Cousin Tirzah. I suppose he thought that since she already had a pack of children, two more wouldn't make any difference. That's where he was wrong.

"Can you pay for their lodging? I got a business to run," Cousin Tirzah said. When the door opened wider, I counted four children. Smirking behind Patience was Eddie. Little Willie darted past in a damp nightshirt. I curiously studied Minnie, who limped around inside the cabin with a rope tied to her foot. Their father was nowhere to be seen.

"Certainly I can pay," Pa replied. "I've got two silver pieces for you. The rest I'll pay in gold when I come back."

"I s'pose you think it's easy to hit pay dirt," Cousin Tirzah snapped. "Ever tried panning for gold on your hands and knees on some no-good placer? A miner with experience can work his way through eleven bushels of dirt, day after day, month after month, and still not find a speck of gold. My husband has been prospecting since April of last year. We ain't got nothing to show for it."

Not acting the least discouraged, Pa rummaged in our wagon until he found a Dr. Wilson Electric Corset left over from his last business. Maybe he figured he'd make Cousin Tirzah happy by giving her a present. Pa loves to give people presents.

"What is this?" Cousin Tirzah asked, holding the electric corset between two fingers as if it were from the Devil himself.

I knew for a fact that the electric deluxe double power belt, which is worn snugly around the waist, was worth five dollars and came with a guarantee to cure back, stomach, and kidney problems, not to mention melancholy and headaches. It seemed the perfect gift for Cousin Tirzah. Instead of acting grateful, Cousin Tirzah threw the corset out the window. All her children, except for Minnie, who was still attached to the table, immediately ran outside to put Pa's gift on the pig.

Eddie laughed whenever the miserable creature squealed.

"S-s-s-stop!" Pheme yelled. "D-d-d-don't hurt that p-p-poor animal!"

Eddie just chased the pig faster.

"Did you tie up your sister?" I yelled to Eddie as he rounded the cabin.

"I didn't tie her up. Ma did. Minnie's being punished for going to visit a neighbor without asking. What's wrong with *your* brother?"

"Nothing," I said defensively.

"He sure talks stupid." Eddie wiped his runny nose along his arm.

Right then, I wanted to haul off and smash Eddie in the face. But I didn't. I had made a promise to Pa to be polite and make the best of our present situation. But I can't help it. Eddie just gives me the nerves when he makes fun of my brother.

Hattie, stop staring into space and help me hang this wash!" Patience says.

Reluctantly, I grab a wet sheet and fling it over the line. We dump the rinse water into the garden. The hot soapy water we use to scrub the kitchen floor. By the time we've finished, I am near exhausted.

"Hey, halfwit!" Eddie yells at Pheme. "Help me stack wood."

Pheme ignores Eddie. He keeps beating a rug on the line. I wish Pheme would beat Eddie instead.

"You heard me, idiot!" Eddie says. He sneaks up, swinging a piece of kindling like he's going to hit Pheme's head.

I pounce on Eddie's back, even though he's taller and heavier than I am. Luckily, I catch him off balance. He stumbles, drops the firewood, and pitches headfirst to the ground. I pin him good and tight with one knee against his neck.

"Take it back! Take it back!" I try to wrench Eddie's arm around behind his waist.

"Won't!" he grunts.

"You will! Take back what you just said about Pheme."

Eddie suddenly twists. I fly into the dirt. He grabs a handful of my hair and shoves my face into fresh horse manure.

"Get offa me!" I scream.

"Say it! Say your brother *is* an idiot," Eddie commands triumphantly. "Admit he don't talk normal. Even Ma says so."

"Your mother is a stinking, skunk-faced liar."

Eddie lets me have another oozing faceful. His sisters cheer. Why doesn't Pheme help me?

"Let me go!" I sputter, and kick wildly.

"What's going on here?" Cousin Tirzah shouts.

Eddie leaps to his feet. "Ma, she called you bad names. So I beat her up."

"Harriet, you are possessed by demons!" Cousin Tirzah yanks me to my feet. "If I weren't such a good Christian, I'd turn you and your slow-witted brother out. Without a roof over your heads or food in your mouths, where would you be, girl, answer me that?" She slaps the only clean place left on my face. I don't give her the satisfaction of seeing me cry or tremble or look away. I want her to know I'm not afraid.

"Mrs. Throckmorton?" interrupts a toothy man in fancy clothes astride a fine horse. Behind him is a short, sad-faced man on foot, holding the reins of three more saddle horses. A pack mule is standing tethered to a tree. "You are Mrs. Throckmorton and this is your lodging establishment, I presume? I am Lord Calvert from London, England. This is my servant, Samuel. I was told our hunting accommodations would be ready when we arrived."

"Certainly, sir!" Cousin Tirzah quickly wipes her hands on her apron.

"Good," Lord Calvert says, carefully removing his fancy gloves and dismounting. "My needs are simple. A good bed, adequate feed for my horses and mule, and three big meals a day served to me punctually. I require fresh trout for breakfast every morning. I hope you can find me the very best trout."

Cousin Tirzah nods. "Yes, I certainly can, sir. But what about the others? I was told there were four servants with you."

"There were four," Lord Calvert says, and sniffs. "But when they learned I planned to track grizzly, three ran away. Only Samuel remained. Good man, Samuel."

Samuel spits a stream of brown tobacco juice into the dirt and frowns.

"I require a good breakfast every day, madam, because I am here to shoot the biggest silver-tipped bear this side of the Rockies. And I do not wish to be disappointed."

"I am sure that you will be satisfied with my lodging and cooking," Cousin Tirzah says. As soon as Lord Calvert disappears to inspect the guest cabin, she pushes me toward the lake. "Go wash your filthy face. When you're clean proper, fill some buckets with fresh water for our guests. Patience can help you. And girl, if you give me any more trouble, you and your brother will be sorry for the day you were born. I warn you."

My head high, I stomp past Pheme. "When are you going to do your own fighting, Pheme?" I hiss, angry that he never came to my rescue. "What happens when I'm not around to protect you?"

Pheme looks down so I can't see his expression. Even so, I can tell he's humiliated. His ears are bright red. I wish I hadn't said those hateful words to him. Maybe Cousin Tirzah is right. Maybe I'm as sinful and worthless as she says.

I join Patience at the lake and splash icy water on my face. When I stand up, I notice someone near the inlet watching us.

"Don't look. Old Judge'll put an Indian sign on you," Patience warns.

"What's an Indian sign?"

"A curse. Don't you know anything?"

"How long's he lived over in that cabin?"

Patience shrugs. "Since before there was a town. He's from out East someplace."

I wave.

"Now what do you think you're doing? Old Judge's a mean, crazy, sinful drunkard and he lives all alone and he's good for nothing. He doesn't respect the Sabbath or the word of God."

"Who says?"

"Ma. She won't forgive me. She says he's responsible for the time Eddie got scarlet fever." Patience sniffs. "All Eddie and his friends done is take some old quilts off Old Judge's clothesline when they wanted to go swimming. Wasn't their fault the lake bed's so rocky."

"What did they do with the quilts?"

"Laid them in the water over the rocks so their feet wouldn't get cut up. Then Old Judge comes running, screaming like a madman. He's shooting his gun and waving willow switches in the air. Old Judge chased Eddie naked as a jaybird all the way home. Next day Eddie caught scarlet fever and it was Old Judge's fault for sure."

I try not to laugh, imagining Eddie hightailing it around the lake without a stitch of clothes.

"Hattie, you coming? I'm not carrying these buckets by myself," Patience whines.

I take one last look. Old Judge casts his fishing line and all of a sudden I get a homesick pang. Sometimes Pa used to go down to the Sangamon River with a bamboo pole and dough balls or soft corn for bait to fish for suckers. Once he took me with him. Made me feel real special.

"Hattie! Stop staring into space and come on, will you?"

I pick up a bucket and follow her. Tomorrow I'm going to try and mail a letter to Pa. Maybe I can convince Mr. Cairns to give me credit for a quarter stamp. How I'll ever pay him back, I don't know. I'll think of some way.

# THREE

The next day, Cousin Tirzah puts me in charge of Willie. Watching Willie is certainly not as bad as doing laundry. Once you get to know him, you realize how different he is from his brother and sisters. They all have mousy brown hair that hangs in limp strings in their faces, except on Sunday when they slick it back. But Willie has brilliant fuzzy yellow hair that looks like spun gold. He likes to smile. And he thinks about all kinds of things. He's real bright, that's for certain. Cousin Tirzah calls Willie a special blessing from Heaven.

One time he stood in the doorway of the cabin and called out, "Hello-hello-hello." Then he turned to me and said, "My word has a shadow."

Today I'm supposed to keep Willie busy while Cousin Tirzah has a cup of tea with Mr. Pug Ryan, who arrived looking as proud as a dog with two tails. And why shouldn't he? He's wearing a soft felt fedora, gold studs on his sleeve cuffs, a big gold ring on his pinky finger, and a shining watch chain looped across his big stomach. Patience told me he owns the Coming Wonder, a gold mine up near Lulu City, about twelve miles from here. That explains why he looks so dressed up and it isn't even Sunday. While I admire his handsome-to-pieces outfit, I don't trust his oily smile. Mr. Ryan looks like he knows something he's not telling—just like the fellow who convinced Pa to sell faulty electric hair-brushes.

I take Willie's hand. We walk to the clearing and settle ourselves not far from the place where Pheme is splitting kindling. I give Willie a spoon to dig in the soft dirt. While he's busy, I take a pencil and a piece of brown packing paper from my pocket and work on my letter.

Dear Pa,

Hope you strike it rich soon so we can build that house with the mahogany banister and send Pheme to Paris to study art. What I want to tell you is we're doing

I pause, trying to come up with the right word. I don't want to tell him how Cousin Tirzah slapped me or the time she made me stay under the bed for bringing a frog in the house. Instead I write:

tolerable. I'm worried about Pheme. He doesn't talk. He doesn't draw. I sure wish you could give me some advice what to do about him. We miss you and your funny stories. I know something will turn up, just like you always say. Cousin Tirzah would sure appreciate a letter or word from

you *soon* saying *exactly* where you are and when you expect to
be coming back for us.

Your loving daughter,
Hattie

I fold the letter and stuff it inside one of the envelopes
Pa gave me before he left. While Willie's busy, I wander
over to my brother. "Pheme, I hope you'll forgive me for
what I said yesterday about not doing your own fighting."

Pheme keeps chopping.

"I am sorry, really I am. It's just that I'm getting worried. Cousin Tirzah told me we have to leave by winter. She
says there won't be enough food for all of us otherwise."

Pheme puts down the ax and wipes his face with his
shirttail. "Pa's g-g-g-oing to w-w-write any day."

"You think so, Pheme?" I'm filled with relief. For a
second, I consider telling him about the letter I intend to
send. Then I change my mind. He'll get angry if he hears
I'm going to borrow money for postage.

Pheme's too proud to beg. I'm not, especially when I
get hungry enough. Back in Springfield it didn't bother me
to go to the butcher's and ask for a bone for our dog, even
though we didn't have one. I knew my brother would boil
that bone to make soup. He's a good cook, even if he's a
boy. Pheme used to take care of me, Pa being gone so much
promoting the benefits of lightning rods around Sangamon
County.

Problem is that hard luck follows Pa whatever new business he tries. He never had what you call formal education.
Pa trusts people. Some of them talk fancy and take advantage
of him. "When you see your neighbor's beard catch fire,"

Pa likes to say, "take water and go and wet your own." But somehow he never follows his own advice. That's how he got saddled with all those electric corsets.

Pheme goes back to chopping. When he bends over to pitch a chunk of wood, I catch sight of his sketchbook sticking out of his back pocket. It's not big—only three by five inches—and the cover's made of genuine morocco leather. Pa bought it for Pheme after he thought he'd strike it rich selling stereoscopes. That sketchbook is Pheme's most precious belonging.

"Can I look at your pictures, Pheme?" I ask quietly. Sometimes when I feel blue, Pheme lets me look at the sketchbook.

He pulls the book from his pocket. Eagerly, I flip to the first page. There she is. The beautiful woman with the dark hair. He's sketched her so lifelike, her hair coiled down her back, her delicate hands folded—

"That's enough," Pheme says. He snaps the sketchbook shut and puts it back in his pocket for safekeeping.

"There's no need for you to grab the picture away so quick. It scares me when I can't recall her face. Does it scare you?"

Pheme's jaw is set, his expression stony. He doesn't like it when I talk about Mama. He turns away and hits a chunk of wood with the ax.

Back in Springfield, I could talk about anything with Pheme. Even about the first day of school and what happened when I wore a cape pinned together from a piece of old red netting. That cape was the prettiest thing, I thought. But all the children laughed at me. Then my teacher asked me what happened to my mulish unruly hair. "Child, why didn't your mother help you?" she asked in front of everyone. I didn't say Pheme had cut most of it off just to get a comb through. I didn't want to feel anybody's pity.

I never liked school much after that first day. Didn't see much point in wasting time trying to make friends with the silly girls my age. They never wanted to do anything interesting like play pirate or flatten nails on the railroad tracks when the Springfield and Northwestern came through. I was happy just tagging after Pheme and his best friend, Miles.

I watch Pheme and sigh. If I lose him, too, what will I do?

Willie and I wander down to the lake. "Tell me stories," Willie demands. He lies down on my apron, which I've spread in the grass, and closes his eyes. One fat finger twitches while he sucks his thumb.

"Once upon a time, a long, long time ago . . ." I begin. When I look down I notice Willie is snoring. A rustling sound in the bushes behind me makes me jump. It's Patience, carrying a sloshing dishpan. "Be quiet! Willie's sleeping," I hiss. "What are you doing?"

"What does it look like? I'm dumping greasy dishwater. Then I'm supposed to go into town for Ma to get a seventy-five-cent bag of sugar," she says, and pulls a scrap of paper from her apron pocket. "This is Ma's mark for Mr. Cairns at the store that means for him to put it on our account." Patience looks at Willie and yawns. "I could sure use a nap, too."

"Well, why don't you sit right down here and rest?" I say kindly. Secretly, I'm inspired. Maybe now I can get to town to mail my letter. "Willie isn't going to wake up for a while. And I'll take care of your errand."

"You will?" Patience asks suspiciously. "Why?"

"Because I like you, Patience." I cross my fingers behind my back so my lie doesn't count.

"You like me?" Her scrawny, homely face screws up in disbelief, as if nobody ever before told her such a thing.

"Sure. Give me the paper and I'll be back in no time."

Patience hesitates, but not for long. "All right," she says.

I grab the note and run toward Last Chance fast as I can. Freight teams and wagons jam Main Street, which is nothing more than two wagon-wheel ruts skirting around tree stumps and boulders nobody in Last Chance has ever bothered to remove. In between the ruts is a muddy path beat by raggedy miners who come to town on burros for provisions.

Mr. Cairns has the only dry-goods business in town. His store is a gray pine board building with two crooked wooden steps, two crooked windows, and a door propped open with a rock. Strays like to sleep in the store's shade and chew on bones thrown out back after Mr. Cairns does butchering.

Out of curiosity, I look over the notices and wanted posters hammered to the store's outside wall. Same stage-coach robbers and horse thieves as last time. The only new notice reads:

MEN AND BOYS NEEDED
AT THE COMING WONDER MINE
*12 hour work day, 3 dollars plus board*
SHOVELERS
MUCKERS
TRAMMERS TO PUSH LOADED CARS
PUMP OPERATORS
*Ask for Pug Ryan, Bucking Bronco Saloon*

A boy with an old man's face and a shabby overcoat stares at the same sign for a minute. I'm real surprised when he quickly scribbles "pinching out" and "underwater" across the bottom with a pencil. He's got two fingers missing. I try not to stare.

"What's that you wrote supposed to mean?" I ask.

"Pug Ryan has hit water," the boy says in a low voice. He looks over his shoulder. "The Coming Wonder is flooding. Anybody who goes to work down that hellhole should be warned they might not get out alive. It's cold, dark, damp, and dangerous. And there ain't no guarantee you'll get your three dollars even if you do manage to climb out. I been there. I know."

Before I can ask more, he turns and shuffles away. I walk inside J. Cairns Dry Goods. The store buzzes with big black flies. Hanging from the ceiling is a board that says "Post Office." Stacked in open crates along the walls are harnesses, plug tobacco, bottles of medicine for mountain sickness, cans of striped candy sticks, and jars of floating pickled eggs. Heaps of miners' woolen pants lean against piles of shirts, gloves, helmets, boots, and mackinaws.

"Hello, Miss Hattie. What can I do for you today?" Mr. Cairns asks. He smacks four flies with a rolled-up *Rocky Mountain News*.

"I need a seventy-five-cent bag of sugar, please." I hand him Cousin Tirzah's note. He scratches his bald head and puts on his glasses. Carefully, he fills a brown paper sack with sugar. "I'll add the sugar to Mrs. Throckmorton's account. Can't say when the last time was I saw her in town. She's a saint, a real saint to have taken you and your brother in. Not many people in her situation would have done the same."

"Yes, sir," I say, wondering what's so saintly about Cousin Tirzah. Nothing I can think of. "Me and my brother are only going to be here for the summer."

"How is Mrs. Throckmorton these days?"

"Tolerable healthy," I reply, hoping to change the subject. "Sir, did any mail addressed to Alexander Phimester and Harriet Elizabeth Proctor come on the last stage from Springfield, Illinois?"

"Let's take a look," Mr. Cairns says. He pulls a wooden canned-goods box from a shelf and thumps it onto the counter. "Help yourself."

I search through a dozen letters and postcards from the Lucky Jack Mine, the Little Orphan, the Belcher, the Highland Mary. I look and look again, but there's no letter from Pa for me and Pheme. I sigh with disappointment.

"This here is a right pretty color one, don't you think?" says Mr. Cairns. He holds a postcard with a three-story brick building and a coach and team in front. "Grand Imperial Hotel in Fairplay. Had this postcard two years now. Sometimes I wonder if I should throw it out. But what if somebody comes in looking for it?"

While Mr. Cairns helps another customer, I turn the postcard over and sneak a peak at the writing on the other side, even though I know I shouldn't. The card is addressed to Phoebe Stevens, Last Chance, Colorado:

DEAR SIS:

THIS IS WHERE I WORK THATS A BIG FLOOR TO WASH AND PLENTY WINDOWS YOU BET I FORGET ONE AND I DONT

GET NO SUPPER ALL WEEK. NO DAY OFF SINCE I COME IM SO
LONLY IF YOU GOT ANY EXTRA I COULD SUR USE SHOES.

Yours truly,

LULITA

Slowly, I tuck the forlorn message back in the box. I
wonder how old Lulita was two years ago and if she ever got
to visit her sister again.

Mr. Cairns lifts the box back on its shelf. "Your pa with
any mine in particular?"

"He's on his own, sir. Pa staked a claim this spring
somewhere in the Neversummer Range. Haven't seen him
since."

"You have a letter ready to send?"

My heart gives a hop. I look at my feet. "I do, but I
haven't got any money to send it."

Mr. Cairns scratches his head. "Tirzah's credit's good."

"No," I say quickly. I don't want more trouble from her
when she finds out. "I'll pay you back myself. I promise."

"Here's a piece of paper and a pencil. Write your IOU."

"Thank you, sir!" I say. I sit down on a crate and write:

HARRIET ELIZABETH PROCTOR PROMISES TO PAY

TWENTY-FIVE CENTS.

Solemnly, I hand him the slip and watch him nail it to
the wall with the others. He puts a stamp on my letter to Pa
and puts it in the box marked "to Gaskill." I feel so happy
and grown up, I decide to try and have a conversation. "You
seem to know most everybody around here, sir."

Mr. Cairns laughs. "Done business with nearly every

freighter, hunter, miner, and fisherman one time or another."

"Even Old Judge?"

"Why would you be asking about him?"

"Only because he's a neighbor, sir," I reply, wondering why talking about Old Judge seems to make everyone around here so hot under the collar. Maybe there's more to him than I thought.

Mr. Cairns takes his time wiping his glasses with a corner of his white apron. "In the old days, when I first came to these parts, Old Judge used to go on regular high lonesomes. He'd get liquored up and wander back in the mountains. Never knew what he did till he came to. I once got Old Judge out of jail in Teller City. He was locked up with three murderers. Told me it was a most humiliating experience. From then on, he's limited his liquoring to one celebration a year—the Fourth of July."

"Doesn't sound like a friendly sort."

"Nobody talks to Old Judge more than he can help it. In my opinion, one finger can't catch a dog flea. It isn't natural for a man to live so alone. He comes in here for supplies maybe once a season. I'd stay out of his way, if I were you. Old Judge prefers his privacy. He calls his side of the lake Paradise."

"What does he call the part where Cousin Tirzah lives?"

"Hell's Gate," Mr. Cairns says, and chuckles.

I smile. Hell's Gate. Cousin Tirzah wouldn't like that, not one bit. Tucking the sugar under my arm, I thank Mr. Cairns for taking my IOU and hurry out the door. Sending a letter isn't as good as talking to Pa, but it's better than nothing. Maybe now Pa will write and tell me and Pheme when he's going to come back for us.

# FOUR

I sprint out of town. Dodging through pine trees, I pause to catch my breath. The branches make this hush-husha noise in the wind, and big black birds call down to me. When I look around, I notice eight gray boards stuck in the ground, eight graves all in a row. I'm surely glad it's not nighttime, because I'd be spooked. I hold my breath, pinch a button on my dress, and walk backward past the cemetery the way I always do to make sure I won't die.

I place the sack of sugar on the ground and explore the grave markers. The first is painted with the words: "Minerva Simonds, died Sept. 10, 1876. Age 75 years, 4 months." Winslow and Lillian Nickerson are next. Beside them is Robert Plummer, "murdered by a gunslinger Christmas, 1877." Doc Duty is fifth. His marker says a snowslide at the Endomile Mine trapped him February, 1878. Next comes Andy Meyers, "struck by lightning digging a well one hot summer day." Seventh is Commissioner John G. Mills, "shot in the back, Fourth of July." Last is a little child. There's no name, no explanation, just "Baby."

I gather a bunch of bright red Indian paintbrush. The flowers make Baby look less forgotten. While I'm picking a pale blue columbine I hear somebody moaning and I run off. Fast as I can, I dash along the lake trail, not stopping once to look back, for fear I'll see a ghost.

It isn't until I'm halfway to Cousin Tirzah's that I convince myself the sound was just the wind. That's when I realize something awful. I left the sugar in the cemetery. By the time I run back, it's too late. The squirrels and camp jays have shredded the brown paper sack and scattered the sweet stuff on the ground. I sprinkle what's left for the ghosts in hopes they'll look kindly on me.

When I return to Cousin Tirzah's, I'm filled with dread. She doesn't believe me when I tell her what happened. She calls me a liar—and worse.

"You're a little, wretched, despicable creature! You're a worm, a mere nothing. You're less than nothing. You're a pitiful insect risen up in contempt against God. When I was your age," she says, beginning the story of her hardscrabble childhood, which is a tale I've heard so many times before, "I earned my living. That was the way I was raised up. I had to get to that button factory by dawn and I never came out again till night. It was hard work. Nobody ever told you about hard work. Nobody ever told you about nothing you need to know. Well, I'm giving you a whipping for your own good. And when I'm through, you are going to pray on your knees for your worthless soul for one hour."

During my whipping, I don't cry. I try not to look sorry.

I know I told Cousin Tirzah the truth. The lie I told had to do with Patience. I don't like her and I never will.

"And don't think I won't make a record of what you owe me for that good sugar," Cousin Tirzah sputters, when my hour is up. She makes a mark in her ledger book. Seventy-five more cents added to our ever-growing debt. "Now get outside and watch Willie. You can help in the garden at the same time."

Eddie, Patience, and Minnie snicker when they see me rubbing my backside. "Hattie, why don't you sit down and rest awhile? Or are you too sore?" Patience taunts. I stick out my tongue at her, but that doesn't make me feel any better. I take Willie's hand. How I wish I could run away from this hateful place.

We crouch beside my brother in the garden. Willie eats dirt while I watch Pheme pulling weeds. "Pheme," I say quietly, and rip out a dandelion so I look busy, "when I was in town, I sent a letter to Pa."

Pheme purses his lips together in a hard, straight line the way he does when he's angry at me.

"It's all right. I signed an IOU for the stamp. I asked Pa when he's coming for us."

Pheme frowns.

"It's not as if we don't trust him. I think we can ask when he's due back, that's all." Now it's my turn to feel angry. Doesn't Pheme realize all the trouble I went through to mail that letter? "Pheme, we have to start thinking about what's going to happen to us. We need a plan. As soon as we find out where he's prospecting, we escape, and go find him."

Pheme's shoulders sag. He shakes his head as if convinced my plan won't work.

"You know what Pa said. 'Get in, get rich, get out.' That's what he intends. So why don't we do the same?"

Pheme stares, mute as an ax handle, and doesn't answer. I'm so mad, I pick up Willie and stomp away before I say something to Pheme I'll regret.

"What are you doing, girl?" Cousin Tirzah demands when she sees me playing chase with Willie behind the cabin. "Satan finds mischief for idle hands. If you're finished in the garden, go to the other side of the lake to the flats and gather some Labrador tea. I need fresh leaves to make tea for Lord Calvert so he can get 'climated. Minnie will show you what the plant looks like."

"All right, ma'am," I say, civil as I can muster. I don't feel the least bit civil. "*Come on, Willie!* Come on, Minnie! You want to come tea-leaf hunting too, Pheme?"

My brother shrugs and follows us, all the time keeping his distance. When I look over my shoulder, he's walking along carving a sharp end on a stick with the pocketknife Pa gave him for his twelfth birthday. Pheme doesn't want us to think he's interested in going to the flats. It makes me crazy when he acts dull as an old gut bucket when all the time he's smarter than the rest of us put together.

"Hattie, gimme a ride!" Willie shrieks, clapping.

I hand the basket to Minnie and kneel on the path so that Willie can climb on my back.

"Horsie! Horsie!" he shouts.

We gallop past town and around the lake. Pheme follows us along the rocky shore. He kicks a rusty can and refuses to answer when we call to him. Minnie points to some small bushes with rosette-shaped leaves. She pulls off a few green, waxy leaves and hands them to me to smell. The fragrance is sweet and reminds me of medicine. It takes a long time to fill the big basket.

I like roaming around the sunny open flats. Grasshoppers leap. The wind blows. I'm reminded of home.

"Watch for snakes!" I warn Willie, whose face is smeared and sticky. He just smiles at me. We wander into the shade of a grove of quivering aspens. The slender trees dance and shimmer. Around the bend I spot someone casting a fishing line. Old Judge.

"If you look at that bad man, he'll shoot you," Minnie says.

"Who says?"

"Eddie."

I should have known.

The rock I throw in the water lands on a bunch of fallen trees jammed against the shore. I throw another. Now there are two rocks side by side, like two passengers on a boat. This gives me an idea. I go farther into the trees. There are all kinds of fallen lodgepole pines helter-skelter among new, younger trees.

"What are you doing, Hattie?" Minnie calls.

"None of your business." I drag a fallen lodgepole down to the water's edge. As I pass, I whisper. "Pheme, you want to help? I'm making a raft."

"Why?" Pheme asks.

I give him a look like he better keep his mouth shut. "No more whippings for me. As soon as we hear from Pa, we'll make our escape across the lake and down the river. Are you going to just stand there or what?"

Pheme wades into the water and arranges logs side by side. Then he takes out his knife and cuts away small branches. I search the woods for more logs, excited to be finally doing something for our escape.

I warn Willie and Minnie not to wander, but they're soon restless. "I wanna go home!" Minnie wails. "I'm bored."

Her complaints make my teeth hurt. "Minnie, pick more Labrador tea."

"I don't want to. You can't make me."

"I'll show you how to weave a necklace with flower stems."

"No. It's too hard. I can't do it. Why are you collecting firewood? We've got plenty at home. I'm hungry." Minnie makes a sour face. "I s'pose you want us to starve."

I sigh. I don't like taking care of Minnie. No matter what I suggest, she is always unreasonable. At least she hasn't figured we're making a raft.

Willie smacks his lips. "Hungry! Hungry! Hungry!"

I don't want to stop working. Can't Minnie and Willie be patient for once? "If you're hungry, just go on home!" I shout.

Minnie stomps away. Willie toddles a few feet behind her. I look over my shoulder as they both disappear among the trees. "Take Willie with you, Minnie!" I call. "Hold his hand!"

Pheme and I work the rest of the afternoon. It takes much longer to build a raft than I thought. We search the forest for long, strong roots. It's past suppertime when we are finally satisfied that the eight logs might hold us.

We have been so busy, I've lost track of time. I haven't

noticed the growing darkness. Across the lake a light bobs. Old Judge's lantern? I shiver. "Let's hide the raft, Pheme. We'd better get back."

Pheme shoves the raft among tall shore weeds. I fumble in the shadows for the basket. What will Cousin Tirzah say when we come home so late? My stomach growls. I'll tell her a bear scared us and then we got lost.

Pheme and I lope through the dark woods. I swing the basket and whistle quietly. We accomplished something important. We built a raft for our escape.

When we reach the clearing near the cabins, I sense trouble. There's Cousin Tirzah motionless in the doorway, her hands on her broad hips. *"Har-riet! Alex-ander Phi-mes-ter!"* she calls shrilly. "You're late. And Willie's not had his supper."

"Willie?" I ask, feeling confused.

"Isn't he with you?"

A cold lake breeze cuts right through me. "No, ma'am," I say slowly. "He came home with Minnie."

"Minnie came home alone. She told me Willie was with you. Where's my baby? You wicked girl, you lost my precious baby! *Will-ie!* Will-ie!" Cousin Tirzah's voice squeaks with panic. She nearly pushes me over as she rushes to the edge of the dark forest and screams, "Will-ie! Will-ie!"

No answer. Eddie, Minnie, and Patience come running from the cabin. "Ma, what's wrong?" Eddie asks.

"Your baby brother's been lost. Eddie, go to Mr. Cairns and tell him we need a search party. We have to look everywhere. Dear Lord, I always knew my angel was too good for this world!"

Pheme and I do not know what to say or do. Cousin Tirzah twists the collar of my dress tight in her fist. "Devil-child, I'll deal with you later. If my baby isn't found alive and well, you can be sure you will feel my wrath and the wrath of God."

## FIVE

My brother and I stumble with a lantern toward the lake. I feel as if I'm in a nightmare, except I can't wake up because I'm not sleeping. This is real. This is terrible. Eerie forest shadows lurk beyond the circle of our lantern's light. All I can think of is poor, beautiful Willie, frightened and lost someplace. Worse yet—dead, just like Baby. And it's all my fault. If only I had not been so anxious to finish that raft! If only I had not sent Minnie away! He never would have disappeared like this.

We search for hours all along the lakeshore. No Willie. The moon comes up cold and gleaming and the sky fills to overflowing with stars. Pheme and I push through the long grass near the place where we hid the raft. No Willie here, either.

I am so miserable and frustrated, I give our raft a good hard kick and break it to pieces. The logs splash and disappear into the dark water. Pheme doesn't try to stop me. I sit down and cry and cry. Willie, beautiful, sweet Willie, is dead and I am surely going to be punished by God and by Cousin Tirzah and I don't know which will be worse. Pheme and I will never escape and nobody will rescue us. My brother reaches out and gives my hair a playful gentle yank as if to say, "It's not so bad." Somehow this only makes me sob louder.

"What's going on?" a voice startles us. "You're upsetting my fish. Why don't you stop blubbering and go home?"

It's Old Judge. I leap to my feet. "We're looking for a lost boy." I quickly wipe my eyes with my sleeve. "Can you help us, sir?" I ask meekly.

"Not you again, Sinner!" Old Judge says. In the moonlight his face looks angry. "Seems you're always asking me for help. Ever noticed that?"

"Please, sir," I beg.

He pauses several moments as if to consider. "Well, all right. If it will mean some peace and quiet. Let's go back to my cabin so I can get my good lantern."

He stomps through the willows. Pheme and I follow. Search party lights blink and jump on the other side of the lake. Voices echo. Waves lap sorrowfully. Maybe I should not have asked for cantankerous Old Judge's help. Why should he care?

"Boss," Old Judge says to my brother as if that were his Christian name, "circle my cabin with your light. Call for that child and step carefully. Sinner, stay put. I'll be right back."

I have no intention of going anywhere, least of all near Old Judge's cabin. Where is his vicious dog? I shiver, wishing I had gone with my brother instead of being left alone in the dark like this.

Suddenly, Old Judge calls out, not loud, not low, "Sinner, come quick!" I'm certain he's found Willie's poor dead body, and I want to run away so I don't have to learn the truth.

"Sinner!" Old Judge calls softly again.

Reluctantly, I walk toward the open cabin door and peer inside. A dozen army muskets, swords, bayonets, and pistols of every shape are stacked above the big stone fireplace. Where is Old Judge? I gulp and glance about the one-room cabin furnished with a pine board table, an old army cot, and a shelf containing more books than I've seen in one place since we left Springfield.

"Where are you, sir?" I whisper.

"Here!" Old Judge is kneeling on all fours near a bundle of beaver pelts and a worn-out quilt on the floor. I step closer. There's Old Judge's dog. And there's a little hand. Oh dear God, did the dog try to eat Willie?

"Come here, why don't you?" Old Judge demands. "I can't see so good. Is this your lost boy?"

Willie's fingers roll into a dimpled fist and crumble a piece of sweet currant cake. His chest moves up and down. Willie, dear, sweet little Willie is alive! That ugly yellow-eyed dog looks up at us, whines softly, and thumps his tail against the hard-packed dirt floor. He seems very pleased with his new friend. Maybe he thinks Willie is half-mongrel, half-coyote, too. "Sinbad, you old varmint!" Old Judge says. "Who said you could entertain a guest while I was out fishing?"

Pheme peers in the doorway. "Come here!" I whisper

hoarsely to him. "We found Willie and he's alive and breathing!" My brother looks relieved. Old Judge picks up the sleeping child and carries him in one arm, his free hand clamped on my shoulder as I lead the way across the footbridge. I walk slowly, carefully following the light from the lantern Pheme holds high.

At the edge of the empty clearing, we wake Willie. He rubs his eyes and walks the rest of the way to Cousin Tirzah's by himself. The minute his mother sees him, she runs tearfully out of the cabin and hugs him to her huge bosom. "Praise be to the Lord!" she says hoarsely, and blows her nose on a flour sack handkerchief. After she's made sure Willie is all right, she peers suspiciously at Old Judge. Then she fixes a stare at me as hard as iron. "Girl, you deserve another whipping for losing Willie like this. I should give your idiot brother the strap, too, just for good measure."

"Pheme didn't have nothing to do with it. It's all my fault, ma'am," I say quickly, hoping that Cousin Tirzah will forgive me and that God will forgive me, too. "No harm's been done. Willie just wandered into Mr. Judge's cabin and fell asleep on the floor. Mr. Judge carried him the whole way here."

Cousin Tirzah's eyes narrow. She turns to Old Judge. "That true?"

He nods.

"Then I'm much obliged to you, sir," Cousin Tirzah says.

Old Judge clears his throat. "This young lady is a vexing inconvenience. I believe a whipping is too good for her."

I take a step back. What does Old Judge mean? "Now you're talking sense," Cousin Tirzah says, and looks as if she's surprised to have something to agree about with Old Judge. "I've never seen such a wayward, disobedient child. Getting out the strap doesn't make any difference. She just goes and sins again."

Old Judge scratches the back of his neck as if he's thinking real hard. Has he got a grin or a frown under that mustache? I can't tell. "Ma'am?" I speak up boldly, hoping there's a way to avoid Cousin Tirzah's whipping after all. "Why not let Mr. Judge decide my punishment? You always tell us the Bible says, 'Work out your own salvation with fear and trembling.' Maybe Mr. Judge has some fearful hard work I can do to pay him back for finding Willie."

Cousin Tirzah's forehead puckers while she considers my penitent idea. "Sounds like a Christian thing to do, except you have to finish your chores here first. No shirking the work I need done. Well, Judge, what will it be?"

We wait for what seems forever.

"Grasshoppers," he says finally.

"Grasshoppers?" Cousin Tirzah replies in a confused voice. "Are you referring to the Bible story about locusts?"

"I'm talking fish bait," Old Judge snaps. "One hundred grasshoppers would do me nicely."

"One hundred grasshoppers?" I ask, never having caught more than five at a time in my life. I take a deep breath. "I'll get you two hundred without any problem."

Old Judge's eyes narrow. "All right, Sinner," he growls, and hurries out of sight.

The next morning I wish I'd never told Old Judge he could pick my punishment. After I finish helping Patience with the laundry, I hurry down to the sagebrush flats with a lard pail and a lid. The grasshoppers are as big and fat as barnyard roosters and twice as ornery. The more I try to scoop up the nasty-looking, yellow-bellied creatures, the more they jump. I use my pail, my apron, my bonnet. They just bounce away.

"Darned hoppers!" I shout.

I need to be patient. I need to be clever. I lie on my stomach in the dust, feeling hot and tired, and wait for the grasshoppers to crawl into the bucket to eat my lunch, a piece of bread smeared with lard. They aren't interested. But I refuse to give up. I invent my own grasshopper sweeper—a long willow branch stripped of all leaves except those on the end. My stick swatter works pretty well at knocking out the grasshoppers long enough to shove them into the bucket before they regain their senses and try to leap away.

When I've counted two hundred I walk to Old Judge's, feeling tired and stiff. Why'd I think this would be easy work? "Hello? Mr. Judge, you in there?"

"Hello, yourself!" Old Judge snarls. He opens the door just a crack. "Didn't I tell you I don't like trespassers?"

"I'm not trespassing. I came here with your two hundred grasshoppers, just the way I promised."

"How do I know there's two hundred in this bucket?" Old Judge says, peering into the lard pail.

"Just ask them."

For the first time, I see Old Judge smile. He tilts his head back and lets out clear laughter that sounds like water running over rocks. "That's a good one," he says, and slaps his leg. He reaches in his pocket and hands me a shining half-dollar.

"What's this for?" I ask, too dazed by the gleaming to be polite the way I should.

"I'm an honest businessman and I'll pay you for the extra hundred. My eyes aren't what they used to be. It would take me a long time to collect that many hoppers. I figure the money's worth it."

I hold the fifty-cent piece tight. Now I can pay back Mr. Cairns and have enough left to send another letter. "You need more grasshoppers?" I ask eagerly.

"Sure," he says. "You're a resourceful gal. I think we can work out a fine business arrangement, don't you?"

I smile and feel very pleased with myself. After all, no one's ever called me resourceful before. I take Old Judge's words as a true compliment.

# S I X

I assure Pheme my grasshopper business is perfectly safe. He's not easily convinced. After we've finished our chores the next day, he follows me to Mr. Cairns's store and watches while I pay the money I owe and send another letter to Pa. "You see? Old Judge's money's just fine," I tell Pheme.

He frowns and trails me to the flats. He watches while I use my hopper sweeper. Once I've collected enough grasshoppers, I set off for Old Judge's. Pheme follows me again.

Ordinarily, I'd be angry at the way he's sticking to me like my shadow. But this time, I'm thrilled. This is the most worried my brother's acted about me since we came here.

The door swings open at Old Judge's place. He surprises me by stepping out with a dozen fishing poles slung over his shoulder. "You caught me just in time, Sinner," he says. He empties my hoppers into a pail he keeps in his cabin. Then he hands me a half-dollar. "Hello, Boss."

Pheme nods and looks uncomfortable.

"Can we help you fish?" I ask boldly, inspired by the fishing poles. Fishing seems a far sight easier than catching grasshoppers. "Pheme and I are the best fishermen in all Sangamon County."

Pheme rolls his eyes. He hates it when I lie.

Old Judge puffs his cheeks like a bullfrog and lets air out slowly. I'm wearing him down, I can tell. I'm good at wearing people down when I put my mind to it.

"All right," he says. "Did you know you are a genuine pest?"

I nod and smile.

"Can you both keep your mouths shut?" Old Judge demands.

Pheme and I promise by crossing our hearts. "Cross our hearts and hope to die, stick a needle in my eye," I say solemnly.

Old Judge disappears inside the cabin and returns with a lumpy gunnysack. He hands the sack to my brother and doesn't say one more word as we start around the lake. The silence makes me nervous. I start thinking, What if I'm wrong? What if Old Judge is as terrible as everyone warned? I haven't seen one yellow cat around his place, only Sinbad and a lame pet crow sleeping in an old boot.

I take my brother's hand. Pheme's jaw is set solid and stubborn. His mouth's a tight line and I know he's trying hard to look brave, even though his hand feels cold and clammy.

"Where you think we're going, Pheme?" I ask in a tiny voice.

My brother doesn't answer.

The cool, damp woods are full of shadows. In a hidden cove Old Judge unties a battered wooden boat. A small puddle of water ripples at one end. I wonder if the boat leaks. I wonder if Old Judge really did give me the Indian sign the way Patience said. Maybe he'll row me out to the middle of the bottomless lake and toss me in because he knows I can't swim.

I think about running away. But where could I go? I pull my hand but my brother holds on tight so I can't escape.

" 'As no man is born an artist, no man is born an angler,' " Old Judge says, and hands Pheme the fishing poles. My brother tilts his head. Maybe he knows what Old Judge is talking about. I certainly don't. Old Judge fumbles for a rope tied around a pine. Hand over hand, he lowers a sloshing bucket suspended overhead. "I keep my bait in a tree in case a hungry bear comes along. Ready to shove off, Sinner?"

I step gingerly aboard, edging past the large wooden box Old Judge heaves on board and fills with water. I take a damp seat at the far end of the boat. Pheme and Old Judge climb in. "Boss, take the oars. Head straight out into the middle, then veer in a southerly direction. Can you see where I mean?"

Pheme nods and begins to row. Old Judge lights his pipe. The sweet smell of smoke suddenly makes me think of Pa, and I wish he could be here with us so I would feel safe. Waves slap against the boat. Pheme breathes hard as he pulls the oars, but he doesn't complain or give up.

This is the first time I have ever been in the middle of the lake. Cool wind whips my hair every which way. I pull my shawl around my shoulders. How much farther? The shore and Cousin Tirzah's cabins have shrunk nearly out of sight. The boat rocks. The fish bait gives off a powerful stink. To keep from thinking about my uneasy stomach, I search the water for signs of trout. I don't want to embarrass myself by throwing up in front of Old Judge and my brother.

"Almost there," Old Judge says encouragingly. Now that we're out in the lake, he sits back. He sings softly, the way a person does who keeps himself company most of the time:

> *When I left the States for gold,*
> *Everything I had I sold,*
> *A stove and bed, a fat old sow,*
> *Sixteen chickens and a cow.*

He pauses and carefully empties his pipe. Pheme lifts the oars, and we drift. "Here is where the fish will bite," Old Judge promises. He opens the sloshing bait pail and hands us each a squirming minnow. I'd prefer to use a grasshopper that's already dead, but I don't say anything because I don't want to appear squeamish.

"I'm only going to say three things and not a word more," Old Judge announces. "Cast as slow and easy as you can. Take up the slack as it drifts so you'll have a tight line. Any trout will hook himself then. And don't horse him in or I'll beat your damned tail off."

I look at my brother and gulp.

"I take fishing seriously," Old Judge says. "This is my livelihood. When I catch a hundred fish, I ship them in a wooden crate by freighter over the pass. Fancy people in Denver restaurants eat my fish. That make you feel important, Sinner?"

I nod. Somehow I'm getting used to my new name.

Pheme and I are not allowed to speak or move about. We have to sit quietly, watching our lines bob in the cold water. When Pa and I fished on the Sangamon, we stuck our poles in the ground and let our lines drift. On shore I could wander wherever I wanted. It's difficult for me to be so calm and patient, sitting in a boat. It isn't my nature. I stretch my cramped legs and straighten my back. If only something would happen!

"Steady, Sinner," Old Judge says softly. "Trout bite when they're ready. 'You will find angling to be like the virtue of humility, which has a calmness of spirit and a world of other blessings attending upon it.'"

Although Pheme seems to understand, I don't have any idea what Old Judge is talking about. But his warning tone is enough to convince me to sit perfectly still for half an hour, staring at the water till my eyes swim. I try to look as calm as I can.

Finally, something tugs on Old Judge's line. The slack goes out and the pole bends. "It's fish! It's fish!" I shout, not the least bit calm. I stand up and nearly topple the boat. Pheme grabs me and makes me sit down.

Old Judge pulls slowly, patiently. A sleek, slim, yellow cutthroat trout leaps out of the water, full of spite and spunk. Old Judge scoops into the net a speckled beauty no bigger than his broad palm. Carefully, he unhooks the fish, lowers it into the water, and lets it go free. "Come again when you grow up."

Pheme's lines quiver. He catches a three-pounder and ten more, right in a row. Each time he and Old Judge put new bait on their lines, hungry trout come calling. All I catch is three fish. Two I have to throw back because Old Judge says they are too small to keep. I am terribly disappointed.

We count eighty fish in the live box. "You two have brought me luck. I think you both could use some vittles after all your labors. An empty bag can't stand up, and a full bag can't bend. A hungry man can't work and an overfed man need not." He takes a loaf of sourdough bread from his sack and tears off a generous chunk for each of us. "I was mistaken, Sinner. You're a good worker when you put your mind to it. And Boss, you seem to be a born fisherman. Do you hunt?"

I nervously take a bite of the delicious bread. The silence seems to go on and on. Old Judge repeats his question, as if maybe Pheme didn't hear him.

"My brother doesn't talk much," I explain, my mouth full.

"I think he can answer for himself," Judge replies slowly. "What do you say, Boss? Do you hunt?"

I hold my breath. This is the first time Old Judge has ever asked a direct question and expected a direct answer of my brother, and I do not know what will happen.

"No. I d-d-don't . . . I d-d-don't . . ." His sentence stops, midstream, like a fish yanked from the water. He struggles hard, closes his eyes, and twists his fingers together. He wants the word to come so badly.

I silently, earnestly pray. *Say it, Pheme. Say it.*

"I d-d-don't have a *gun!*" he finally explodes.

Most grown-ups who hear my brother stutter badly for the first time always look away, as if watching him talk is too painful. But Old Judge doesn't seem the least bit embarrassed for my brother. His expression shows no pity, no scorn. He stares directly at Pheme when he says, "Boss, would you like to learn to shoot?"

Sweat glitters on Pheme's forehead. He bites his lip.

"Well, if he doesn't want to learn to use a gun, I'd like to," I interrupt. Hunting is unladylike, I know. But I have never thought of myself as much of a lady. Besides, if I could hunt, maybe I might make us a fortune. I've read about trick sharpshooting women, the kind who make hundreds of dollars performing in the circus. They balance atop a fat white mare and shoot teacups off people's heads. Maybe I could do that. Maybe I could be famous. Maybe I could be rich.

"I can teach you to hunt, too, Sinner. But I'm asking your brother," Old Judge says, turning to Pheme. "Would you like to learn to shoot?"

"Yes. B-b-but P-P-Pa took the only g-g-g-un."

"I've got plenty of guns. Enough for both of you."

The grim, straight little line that Pheme's mouth usually is suddenly relaxes. The shadow of a grin flits across his face.

"Do we have to go back?" I ask Old Judge.

"We can wait a bit, if you'd like to try casting your lines again," he replies, and offers us another chunk of bread and a cool drink of water from his canteen. When we're finished eating, Old Judge settles in for a good, long smoke. Pheme baits his hook and lets it fly. The plop of his line in the water echoes loud and clear.

Boat water drifts around my feet. I wiggle my toes and decide to try and make adultlike conversation. "Mr. Judge?"

"Call me Saint J.L., Sinner."

If we have made-up names, I suppose it's only fair for him to have one, too. "What does 'Saint J.L.' mean?" I ask.

Old Judge blows a ring of smoke. "The 'J' stands for Joseph, my humble first name. The 'L' is for my middle name—Lyle. My mother had the foresight to name me after her brother, Lyle, who later shocked the family by disappearing down the Nile on some African expedition."

"But what about the Saint part?"

"Inspired by a favorite poem by Matthew Arnold. Maybe you know it, Boss? 'Strong is the soul, and wise, and beautiful: / the seeds of godlike power are in us still: / Gods are we, bards, saints, heroes, if we will.'"

My brother nods. He knows the poem, I guess. I watch a ring of smoke float toward heaven and ask, "Saint J.L., have you ever seen anyone drown?"

My brother shifts uneasily in his seat and gives me a dark look, as if to ask, What kind of polite talk is this?

"I'll tell you a story. It was 1869, I believe. Watch your line, Boss." Old Judge leans back and shuts his eyes. "When I came here, I was one of the first white men this side of the range. I learned to respect this lake. It has a power and spirit all its own. Some early-spring nights, I'll wake up thinking I'm hearing music. Chopin piano concertos. Violin sonatas by Vivaldi. But it's Lone Squaw, half-frozen, half-thawed, moving and shifting under the weight of ice."

"Yes, but what about the drowning?" I ask impatiently.

"I'm getting to that, Sinner. The first summer I built my cabin, the two Cole brothers came here. Neither had much respect for the lake. They came to fish as much as they could. They built a raft, floated out, and started to fill their creel."

I squirm, thinking about our raft in pieces somewhere.

"As luck would have it, a storm came up. Hadn't much in the way of paddles. It took them a while to fight against the waves and move toward shore. One of the boys could swim. He thought he'd be better off jumping in. But it didn't take long for him to be seized with cramps in the icy water. Never found his body."

"What happened to his brother?" I quickly pull my hand out of the water for fear of touching old bones or a skull with hair.

"His brother? Well, he didn't know what to do. This was fortunate. He just held tight to that raft. The sky flashed with lightning, rain fell, and the waves rolled white. Eventually, he was blown to safety on the east shore. That's where I discovered him—alive, but only barely."

Nervously, I move to the middle of my seat. I'm glad Pheme and I did not try to float away on our own makeshift raft.

"That was years ago. I've never told that story to anyone. Of course, nobody ever asked me." He stares quietly into space. "Come to think of it, I can't remember the last time I went fishing with anyone. My habit is to go alone."

"Well, how do you like it?" I ask.

"Like what?" Old Judge says, puzzled.

"How do you like fishing with us? Can we do this again?"

Old Judge laughs. "I know better now not to say no to you, Sinner. Especially when you have that determined look in your eye. Let's put our backs to it, shall we? It's time to head for shore. Sinbad's going to wonder where I've been."

The mist lifts and I can see the shore again. Old Judge

takes one oar, Pheme the other. At the top of his lungs, Old Judge sings "Seeing the Elephant." The words and melody bounce off the rocky cliffs and dark trees. The only songs I know are hymns. But I like Old Judge's song and put my favorite verses to memory. At the chorus, I join right in:

> On the Platte we couldn't agree,
> Because I had the di-a-ree;
> We were split up, I made a break,
> With one old mule for the Great Salt Lake.
> So leave, you miners, leave
> Oh leave, you miners, leave!
> Take my advice, kill off your lice,
> Or else go up in the mountains!

Pheme dips the oar to help keep time. Pretty soon, he's harmonizing right along with Old Judge and me. As loud as we can, the three of us let our voices ring out the terrible, disgraceful lyrics all the way back to shore.

# SEVEN

Just in time for our noon meal!" Lord Calvert announces in his loud, musical voice as soon as he spots Pheme and me coming through the woods with a string of twenty fine trout. "Now *those* fish look delightful, Mrs. Throckmorton. A far cry better than the scrawny, bony perch you served yesterday."

Cousin Tirzah nods to her guest. "I'll have them cleaned and fried in no time, Lord Calvert. You'll have a proper breakfast." She turns a stern, questioning glance in my direction. "Where were you?"

"Old Judge's. We helped him fish. He gave us these to keep."

"You better not be lying, girl. What happened to those grasshoppers you promised?"

"I gave them to him, ma'am. He said he'll pay me half a dollar for every hundred I catch from now on. He said we can help him fish anytime you'll let us. When we do, we can bring home part of the catch."

"Old Judge told you that?" Cousin Tirzah replies. "Was he sober or drunk?"

"Sober, ma'am."

Cousin Tirzah shakes her head in disbelief.

"Before I forget, madam," says Lord Calvert. "I have a letter for you. I picked it up at the general store when I was inquiring about my money order."

Cousin Tirzah thanks Lord Calvert. She glances briefly at the greasy yellow envelope and slips it inside her pocket. Why doesn't she open it right away? I wonder. She's never received a letter before. It's only after the dishes are washed that she corners me. I flinch, thinking she's changed her mind and she's going to slap me for staying so long at Old Judge's. For some reason, she doesn't.

"Hattie, I've a mind to hear what's in this letter." She takes the envelope from her pocket and puts it on the table.

I look at her curiously and feel relieved. Maybe now I have an excuse to escape. "I'll leave the cabin if you want to be alone."

She shakes her head. "That's not what I mean. I'm asking you— What I mean is—" She sighs, her face flushed.

That's when I realize Cousin Tirzah can't read. I pick up the envelope and open it. For the first time there's something I can do for Cousin Tirzah that maybe she'll appreciate. I clear my throat.

June 30, 1882

Dear Mrs. Throckmorton:

I am writing to tell you unfortunate news. On Tuesday the sixteenth of last month Mr. Throckmorton passed away when a dynamite blast went off unexpectedly. There was nothing we could do for him. He is with Jesus in Heaven in everlasting peace—

Cousin Tirzah sinks into a chair. She's so pale, you'd think she was ill. Eddie bursts into the room. Behind him creeps Pheme. "We're finishing Horse Thieves and Vigilantes," Eddie says breathlessly. "Hattie, you coming out? What's the matter, Ma?"

Cousin Tirzah doesn't answer.

Eddie glances suspiciously at me and then at the paper in my hand. "What happened?"

"Your pa died," I tell him softly. "I'm sorry." Eddie just stands there, stunned, as if he doesn't hear me. "Cousin Tirzah, you want me to read the rest?"

Cousin Tirzah nods.

" 'We gathered what remains we could after the blast,' " I continue, " 'and buried him here in Telluride. We only discovered your whereabouts last week. Otherwise we would have told you right away. The burial costs were $24.30. If you can see your way clear to send cash—' "

Eddie whirls and faces me. "I wish you never came," he snarls. "This is all your fault. You and your halfwit brother. If you never came, things would be just as they was. Pa'd still be alive. Even Ma said you've been nothing but bad luck and heartache. Isn't that right, Ma?"

Cousin Tirzah stares off into space, barely breathing.

Eddie curls his fists and spins, like he's got to do something, hurt somebody in the worst way to shake off the terrible news. He slams Pheme against the wall. "I'll show you!" Eddie shouts. He grabs Pheme's sketchbook from his back pocket and dashes out the door.

For a moment, I'm too shocked to do anything. When I recover my senses, I hightail it after Eddie. "Come back here!" I scream.

Eddie is all the way out of the yard and running up the road. I pump my legs as hard as I can, but they don't move fast enough. Eddie rounds the bend. Where's he going? He's made it past the trees, almost to the bridge. The river! He's going to the river!

I run faster. He pauses and looks over his shoulder at me. The look he gives me sends chills down my spine. In one huge arc, he hurls Pheme's precious sketchbook into the thundering spray.

"No!" I scream.

I skid to the river's edge, breathless, horrified. The brown leather notebook bobs under a curling white lip of water and vanishes. Downstream, it reappears. The notebook floats! I leap to a rock, then another. I reach. The notebook swirls away. Icy spray soaks my dress, my face.

Where is it? I spot the sketchbook wedged between a split boulder—beyond any other stepping-stone I can reach in one leap. I lower myself into the deep calm water, smooth as green glass. My ankles, my knees go numb. I keep moving. If I don't grab the sketchbook before the falls, it'll be gone for good. Just as I'm about to make the grab, my foot slips.

I plunge headfirst. Arms waving wildly, I struggle for breath. Frantic to find a toehold, I pull myself onto a fat boulder. When I look, the sketchbook has drifted away. I struggle downstream, crawling atop boulders, searching twisted fallen branches. Where did it go? The roar of the falls is so loud, I can feel the earth shake under my feet. I'm about to give up when I spot something brown trapped in a

tangle of an uprooted bush caught in the current maybe four
more yards downstream.

Scrambling faster, I jump from rock to rock. The water
moves faster, whiter, chanting. The dizzy current flows over
the tops of boulders, pushing, curling. I stumble and fall.
The current catches me and pulls me under. Pebbles scrape
my back, my arms. My head throbs. I gasp for air. The
sky below, the water above. I am pushed under the dark
green water. Coughing, sputtering, I burst up for air. I spin.
Tumble upside down. I make a grab for a dark shape—a
passing rock—and am pulled away. I go under again.
The roar. I can hear the tumble of water, the sound of the
falls.

The current slams me against something solid. I lift my
head, breathe. There! I dig my fingernails into the slime-
covered rock. Slipping, slipping. I see something beneath a
branch. Make a reach for it! Make a—

I grab. My fingers curl around something. But the rock
slips away. I am sucked under. White water, endless spinning moving chanting pulse. Better to drift, to slip away
under the icy green.

Something yanks my arm. I'm hoisted into bright light.
My legs and arms ache. I'm coughing hard. Harder. Suddenly, I'm hearing Mama again. That terrible coughing that
never stopped. We're back in Illinois. I want to open my
eyes but I can't. I hear voices. Familiar voices—

"Consumption," the doctor says. "Take her to Colorado
and give her the camp cure."

Now I can see Mama. But she's blurry. Her face is pale
and thin with enormous black mirror eyes. She's propped
up on a hill of pillows in a dark bedroom, surrounded by

funny-smelling tonics and elixirs Pa bought on credit, hoping to make her better. Pa loads her in the wagon, along with his mining outfit of pickaxes, shovels, sheet-iron mining pans with copper bottoms. There's a shadowy smile on her face, as if she really believes the camp cure will work.

We're in Ogallala, Nebraska. The big trees are yellow, so yellow. I'm standing in a cemetery. The wind's blowing hard. We don't know anyone there and I don't want to leave Mama with so many strangers. Something's in my hand. I hold tight. I won't let go. I won't leave. I won't—

"Hattie!"

I open my eyes wide and blink in bright light.

Pheme crouches on the ground beside me. I must still be alive. His expression is so worried, so anxious. He brushes away hair that's plastered over my eyes, my mouth. When I look down at my hand I'm surprised. There, gripped tight, the sketchbook. Maybe I'll never be able to uncurl my fingers again.

My brother manages to pry the book loose. He opens it. Water drips from the pages. "The pictures," I whisper hoarsely. "Are they ruined?"

Pheme flips through the soggy pages. Since he could only afford pencil, not ink, nothing has been lost. Some of the drawings are smeared but most are still visible. He smiles and wipes the leather cover on the back of his pants. I sit up, thinking I'm a real hero. Then I reach inside my pocket.

"Oh, no!" I burst into tears.

"Y-y-you hurt?" Pheme asks, his face filled with concern.

"No!" I wail. "I lost my money in the river!"

Pheme puts his hand on my shoulder and gives me a pat. Just like the old days. "I'll help you hunt m-m-m-ore grasshoppers," he promises.

I look up at him and smile. That's the longest sentence he's said aloud since we've come to Colorado.

# EIGHT

Dear Pa:

Did you get my other two letters yet? Yesterday Pheme and I went high up into the mountains to the place where it's too cold for trees to grow. If I stretched my arms, I thought I could touch the sun. Faraway peaks melted deep purple to pale gray and wind made shivers through the tiny yellow flowers and bright firewood. That meadow was as colorful as Mrs. Penway's garden back home. I didn't know mountains could be so beautiful.

We saw some elk. Pheme has it in his head to get himself some antlers. There's somebody here who says he'll teach Pheme to shoot, only I don't see how since the fellow's half blind. I like him, though. He lends me books. I'm reading *Gulliver's Travels,* which is an exciting adventure story that you would enjoy.

You can be sure I was surprised when I woke up the other night and spied Cousin Tirzah drying Pheme's sketchbook over the stove and then pressing each page with a flat-iron as if it was a fine tablecloth. Maybe she felt bad that Eddie threw it in the river. Or maybe she just liked the pictures.

Sorry this is such a long letter but I want to get my postage's worth. Maybe you already heard from other miners about Mr. Throckmorton's accident. Cousin Tirzah's children don't seem so put out that their father's never coming back. Maybe because they hardly knew him. He wasn't home much.

That's the only news. *Please write to us.*

I sign my name and fold the letter into its envelope. I stretch. Where I'm sitting beside the swinging sheets is warm and sunny. I put the letter in my pocket and close my eyes to take a short nap. All of a sudden, I hear Cousin Tirzah talking to somebody. I creep on my hands and knees behind a washtub.

". . . must be a heavy responsibility for you," a deep, unfamiliar voice says.

"I'm only trying to discharge my duties faithfully in the sight of God," Cousin Tirzah replies, and sighs loudly.

"As I said before, our lives are full of trials and suffering. I've got a big problem up at the Coming Wonder. The shaft's filling with water because of seepage from underground springs. It's a promising vein, if I can just get somebody small enough down there to bail out. None of my other workers will do it. They say it's too dangerous."

"It's a sorry world we live in, when people can't be satisfied with an honest day's work. You say Nellie Meltzer's got fifty-four rooms at the Grand Imperial Hotel in Fair-play?"

"That's right. It's a fine hotel, but she can't keep good help either. If you accept my offer, I could help take the burden of those children off your hands and help you invest a tidy sum of your own. A woman like you needs to think about the future. There's no law that says you have to spend the rest of your life like this."

Cousin Tirzah clears her throat. I suspect she's noticed my feet sticking out from behind the washtub. "Harriet! Come over here!"

Cautiously, I come out of my hiding place. There's Pug Ryan tilting back on the tall heels of his shining boots, his thumbs hooked in his vest pockets. "This is the girl?" he asks.

Cousin Tirzah nods. She smiles unpleasantly at me so the window gaps in her mouth show.

"Girl, what's your name?"

"Harriet Elizabeth Proctor, sir," I mumble. So I don't have to look at his eyes, I stare at his enormous gold watch chain.

"When I was your age I earned my own living. I had to get to that button factory by dawn and I never came out again till nightfall. This was the way I was raised up . . ." Cousin Tirzah drones on and on while I study Mr. Ryan's gold chain. ". . . I look back upon a martyr's life of toil, and privation, and pain, and I am ready for a martyr's death," Cousin Tirzah says, and pauses to take a breath.

"A-men!" Mr. Ryan says. He thrusts his fleshy fingers into his pocket. Just as I hoped, out comes the beautiful watch, shimmering in the sunlight. He flicks the lid open.

Music twinkles as if by magic. When he sees me smiling, he snaps it shut. The music stops. "I must be on my way. If you're as clever a woman as I think you are, you'll consider my proposal seriously, Mrs. Throckmorton. I'll wait only so long. There are many other women just like you who'd jump at the chance."

"Good-bye, Mr. Ryan," Cousin Tirzah calls as he rides away in a two-wheeled carriage drawn by a fine white mare.

I watch in amazement. There are nearly twenty men for every woman in Last Chance, Mr. Cairns once told me. Even so, I can hardly believe that Mr. Ryan's gone sweet on Cousin Tirzah! Does every bachelor in the territory know she's a widow? I wonder. And why would anyone as grandly dressed as Mr. Ryan want to propose to ill-tempered Cousin Tirzah? Hasn't he noticed she wears dresses made from feedsacks dyed black? Must not bother him one bit, if he plans to take her on a honeymoon trip someplace as fancy as the Grand Imperial Hotel in Fairplay.

I decide to tell Pheme the news and ask what he thinks. As soon as I reach the shed where he's been stacking wood, Pheme bolts into the woods like his pants are on fire. I follow him. Just as I suspect, he heads right for Old Judge's place. I keep my distance and hide behind a tree.

Old Judge opens the door to his cabin and peers out. I'm thinking Pheme won't have enough courage to argue Old Judge into setting up target practice the way he promised. I can't hear what either of them is saying, so I creep closer. Pheme looks nervous. Pretty soon, there's Old Judge carrying old tin cans. He hands them to Pheme and points to the crumbling wall behind his house. Without thinking, I walk out of my hiding place. "Pheme, what do you suppose you're doing?"

"He's learning to shoot, that's what," Old Judge snaps. He doesn't look especially happy to see me. "Sinner, are you always so nosy about your brother's business?"

I don't like his comment but I try not to let that show. With my hands on my hips, I demand, "Sir, you said you'd teach me, too."

"That's right, I did." Old Judge fills the cans with water. I want to ask him why, but I don't, because I don't want to irritate him any more than I already have. He carries four ancient, deadly guns from his house. "This is a Spencer carbine, a breech-loading repeater I happen to know was used on the first day of the Battle of Gettysburg," he says. "It was the best military weapon available during the war. I named this gun Old Satan."

"You were a soldier?" I ask. Old Judge gives me this look like he didn't hear me. I know he doesn't want to talk about it, so I don't repeat my question.

"Now I'll show you how it works," Old Judge says. He takes a handful of copper-covered cartridges from his pocket and loads them into an opening he calls the magazine, located in the rifle's butt stock. "The rifle is ready to fire when a cartridge has been fed into the firing chamber. What happens when you aim the rifle and squeeze the trigger is that the firing pin strikes the rear end of the cartridge and ignites primer. The primer in turn sparks a fire inside the cartridge's propellant powder. That burning powder creates pressure and drives the bullet spinning hell-bent-for-leather down the barrel."

He shows how to push down on the rifle's lever to release a used cartridge. Lowering the breechblock near the trigger makes a spring inside the rifle shove a fresh cartridge into place. Old Judge says that when he raises the lever, the breechblock comes into contact with the new cartridge and pushes it smack into the barrel and then closes the breech. I just concentrate on the part about cocking the hammer and pulling the trigger.

"Ladies first, Sinner. Would you care for a few more instructions?" Old Judge hands me the enormous gun, which is so heavy I can barely hold it.

"Shooting's easy. Anyone knows that," I brag. "I've done it loads of times. All you have to do is point the thing in the right direction."

"There's more to it than that. Why don't you let me show you—" Before Old Judge can finish, I take aim at the cans. The gun blasts, kicks back, and knocks me flat on the ground.

"Are you all right?" Old Judge looks worried.

"I'm fine," I lie, and rub my poor shoulder. I know I'll be bruised for a week. It's then and there I decide I don't want to join the circus as a lady trick sharpshooter. It hurts too much.

Pheme doesn't seem discouraged.

"The first step in becoming a good shot is *wanting* to be a good shot. Know what I mean, Boss?" Old Judge says.

My brother nods seriously.

"Steadiness, steadiness. That's the ticket. Control the trigger and get the shot off properly. Start out shooting from the steadiest possible rest. Watch me." Old Judge grunts a bit, lies on the ground on his stomach, his left elbow under the rifle. He sights his target. "Up in the mountains you can assume a prone position to shoot moose or grizzlies in a basin below."

I stare wide-eyed at my brother, trying to imagine him shooting some big, man-eating bear, not just a row of creamed-corn cans. Pheme lies on his stomach and takes careful aim.

"The thing to remember is never rest your rifle barrel over anything hard or your shot will fly high. Pad the rifle over stones or logs with a jacket or a hat so it won't recoil," Old Judge says, studying my brother's form. "Remember, squeeze that trigger gently. Don't think about the gun going off. Concentrate on the squeeze. Aim will come naturally."

Pheme misses twice and nicks the cabin wall once. I don't feel so bad about how poorly I did.

Old Judge is practically jumping up and down. "Don't yank the trigger, Boss! Concentrate! Concentrate! Take a deep breath, exhale part of it, and don't breathe again until you've fired. Relax a minute and then try again."

Pheme wipes his sweaty face with his shirtsleeve. Slowly, he takes a deep breath and makes a little whistling sound through his teeth. His lips close. He raises the rifle sight on his elbow and pulls the trigger.

*BOOM!* The can explodes. Old Judge laughs and slaps his knee. I cheer. Now I know why he filled those cans. The weight keeps the cans steady. And it's more exciting when the water splats and goes flying after a direct hit.

"Can you remember exactly where your sights rested when the gun went off?"

Pheme shrugs.

"Next time, call the shot. Increase your trigger pressure when the sights look right, slack up when they don't," Old

Judge says. "Now I'll show you the sitting position. It's not as steady as the first I showed you, but it's good to use when you're after something big and you've got to make sure your shot hits the mark."

"You mean, if he's being chased by a fierce mountain lion or something?" I ask.

"Why not?" Old Judge says. "Here's how it looks. Sit like this, about forty-five degrees from the line of aim. Lean well forward and put the flat of your left elbow against the flat of your left knee. See what I've done? I've made a solid shooting platform."

"You mean, with his legs crossed like this?" I do a silly Indian-style demonstration of my own. Sitting in the dirt doesn't seem right. It's not dignified. I'm sure gun-toting vigilantes don't fold up their legs like grasshoppers. They stand proud and deadly whenever they blast horse thieves to pieces.

Pheme follows Old Judge's directions, positioning his wobbly elbows on his wobbly kneecaps.

"Don't sit too straight, Boss. Keep your feet and ankles relaxed and well apart. The harder you try to hold the position, the more tense you'll become. The more tension, the more wobble."

"When's he going to learn how to shoot standing up on his hind legs?" I ask.

"Soon enough," Old Judge answers, not even looking at me. "It's better to get one well-aimed shot from the sit than to get in four poorly aimed, poorly held, poorly placed misses offhand."

"Oh," I say, feeling small and hurt. I rub my shoulder and make a sad face but nobody notices. Hoping to get the attention of Pheme and Old Judge, I announce, "I know something neither of you do. Mr. Ryan, who wears fancy clothes and has a big gold watch that plays music, came all the way from his mine today to make Cousin Tirzah a serious proposal. He wants to marry her! I heard the whole thing. What do you think about that?"

Old Judge roars with laughter.

"What's so funny?" I feel hurt that he thinks my marvelous news is just a big joke.

"Pug Ryan is the last man on earth who'd marry Tirzah. I'll bet the hair on my head he came crawling from his mine near that whooping, sleepless, gold-drunk camp near Lulu City to see if she'd grubstake him on another claim. He must be desperate for cash. Sinner, it's not ladylike to eavesdrop." Old Judge winks.

I blush bright red and wander into the front yard of the cabin. To keep occupied, I throw sticks for Sinbad.

BLAM . . . BLAM . . . BLAM . . . BLAM . . . BLAM . . . BLAM . . . BLAM!

"Hey, Sinner!" Old Judge yells. I come running, wondering if my brother shot his foot. But there he is, standing next to Old Judge, looking proud and happy. "How do you like that? Boss shot five out of seven targets. Not bad, is it?"

"Not bad," I say, feeling proud and happy, too. "Congratulations, Pheme!"

Pheme quickly reloads. For the first time in ever so long, there's a real, honest-to-goodness smile on his face.

# NINE

**G**irl, where've you and your brother been?" shouts Cousin Tirzah as soon as she sees us coming through the clearing. She's standing in the yard with Eddie, Minnie, and Patience. Mr. Cairns's ornery horse, Folly, chews the few green stems of grass pushing up around the main cabin.

"We were just in town to mail a letter and check the Thursday mail delivery," I say proudly, hoping that she's impressed by the fact that I can pay for postage myself with my grasshopper money.

"Any letter from your pa?" she demands impatiently.

I shake my head.

Cousin Tirzah snorts as if she'd expected just that. "You're wasting time. I need you to help with the packing. You're going wild-raspberry picking."

"Raspberry picking! Who's going?" I ask, surprised and delighted to be allowed to slip away from endless cabin chores.

"You, Eddie, Patience, Minnie, and that brother of yours," Cousin Tirzah says. "I've got eight empty lard buckets collected. I want them all filled when you get back. I expect you can feed yourself trout as you camp."

I'm pleased Pheme and I will have a chance to show off the fishing skills Old Judge taught us. I give an anxious sideways glance at Eddie. I figure I better try and make peace with him, even though he's the one who nearly got me drowned. Cousin Tirzah's told him he can take along his father's old muzzle-loader on our berry-picking trip. That's another reason I'm feeling nervous. What does Eddie know about guns? I figure it's better to be friends than enemies with somebody who's carrying gunpowder and shot.

I see my opportunity as we're gathering wood to fill the wood box beside the stove. "I am sorry about your pa, Eddie," I say in a low voice. "I know just how you must be feeling."

"No you don't," Eddie replies, and picks up three logs. "I don't want to talk about it."

"Fine," I tell him. Since he doesn't try to hit me with the firewood, I suspect he's not angry anymore. It's all right with me if I never mention Mr. Throckmorton's name again as long as I live. "Where's this place with the raspberries, Eddie?" I ask, trying to change the subject.

"Up eight miles on Dawson Creek, not far from Sowbelly," Eddie says. "Just got to make sure to watch for bears." Eddie grins when he sees my jaw drop as we come into the kitchen. "Bears like raspberries, too."

"Ma, what about Willie?" Minnie asks. "Is he coming?"

Cousin Tirzah shakes her head. "He's staying here with

me where he'll be safe. I'm expecting company. Your chores will be waiting for you when you get back."

"That Pug Ryan again," Eddie grumbles. "When's he going to stop coming around?"

"What did you say?" Cousin Tirzah demands.

"Nothing, ma'am," replies Eddie.

"Well, finish packing," Cousin Tirzah says.

Patience finds an old canvas wagon sheet that has six holes to the square inch. Pheme collects fishing tackle and a moth-eaten blanket. Minnie digs up an old frying pan, a few tin plates, tin cups, and old knives her mother doesn't need. I collect our food supplies, which aren't much. A piece of salted pork, a few loaves of bread, a bit of salt. I hope the fishing's good, or we may starve. Eddie collects matches, which he slips inside two cartridge shells fitted together. He says it's a cowboy trick he learned to keep the matches dry. I tuck the matches in my pocket for safekeeping since I know Eddie's attraction to moving water.

Bright and early the next day, we load the horse we borrowed from Mr. Cairns. The buckets clang and clatter as potbellied Folly starts out. "Be careful and watch out for fire," Cousin Tirzah calls, trying to keep Willie from running after us. He cries and cries at being left behind. But Cousin Tirzah doesn't look sad we're leaving. She's got a red geranium blossom pinned to the shoulder of her best black Sunday-go-to-meeting dress, and it's not even Sabbath yet.

My job is to walk in front with the horse's reins and make sure he doesn't have one of his spells. When Folly has a spell, he sits in the road and rolls over. We're all in high spirits. Even Pheme has found a walking stick and he seems to have kind of a bounce in his step. For once, Eddie doesn't try to start a fight. He carries his father's old muzzle-loader proudly over his shoulder. I can't help feeling nervous when the barrel points my way.

The air feels fresh and cool. Overhead the sky is clear and blue and the forest is fragrant with pine and juniper. When we leave the road and start across a shallow creek to reach the inlet trail, the horse refuses to budge. We have to coax him across to get his feet wet. As we climb higher along the trail, we move more slowly. My face sweats. The sun burns the top of my head and my shoulders. The only sound is the cling-clang of the berry buckets and the horse's hooves biting the dry dust.

The path becomes steeper. In the thin air, I have to use all my energy just to put one foot ahead of the next. Finally, we stop and I can catch my breath. Branches moan and squeak in the wind. I spot a pine with bark strangely scratched and torn and stretch on tiptoe to reach the tree's scar. Five marks match my five fingers. "What's this?" I ask Eddie.

"Grizzly claw," he replies. "Not full grown."

"One that's grown stands nine feet tall on his hind legs," says Patience with authority.

I shiver. The mark looks fresh. What if the grizzly is still nearby?

"See any sign of Ute Indians?" Minnie asks in a small voice. She has climbed on the horse's saddle after complaining that her bare feet hurt too much to walk.

"We'll keep a lookout," I tell her. I don't think anybody's seen any Indians in this part of the territory for some time, but I don't want to scare her—or myself—with such talk.

"Don't worry," says Eddie. "I've got a gun and I'm a dead shot."

I try not to look at Pheme, because I'm afraid I'll start to laugh.

"How much farther?" Patience complains. "I'm dreadful tired. When we going to have something to eat?"

"Soon as we reach the stream," says Eddie. "Then we'll catch some fish and fry them. We don't want to stop here where there's bear signs. A grizzly might smell us and come looking for dinner."

Minnie whimpers. "Do bears eat people?"

"Lord Calvert told me they do," says Eddie in a gleeful voice. "I don't think we should take any chances, since you're so nice and fat."

Minnie bursts into a howl. "Shut up, Eddie," Patience says. "You'll make her hystronical."

"Anybody know a good song?" I ask, hoping to avoid a fight. "How about this one?" I teach them Old Judge's song and they especially like the part about the di-a-ree. We reach our camp a little past noon. The raspberries hang like jewels. We hobble the horse so he won't run off. While Eddie, Patience, Minnie, and I climb over rocks and logs with a bucket in each hand to pick berries, Pheme sets out for the stream with the fishing pole.

The sun feels warm on our backs and everything seems still and peaceful. Once the bottom of my pail is covered, it takes ever so long to fill. The last inch is the slowest. But we all fill our first buckets knowing we can eat the sweet raspberries with fried fish.

By the time we return to our camp, Pheme has a good fire going. He's cleaned three mountain trout and he's frying them in a pan. Even Eddie seems impressed that my brother made such a fine catch—a total of six speckled beauties. We're all nearly starved and our faces and hands are sticky with red berries.

"Ma will be surprised when she sees all the buckets filled," says Patience. "We'll cook up some jelly, maybe some cobbler."

We eat in silence till every bit of bread and fish is gone. Pheme insists we burn the bones so that a bear won't come looking. He and Eddie set up a tent, throwing the piece of canvas over some bent willows. They secure the ends with rocks.

"We've still got four more buckets to fill before we can go home," Patience announces. "We'll have to go up the hill to pick some more." Her sister and brother groan.

"What's up the hill?" I ask.

"You mean, what *was* up the hill," says Patience.

"What do you mean?"

"Name of the town was Sowbelly. There was big diggings up that way that never panned out," says Eddie.

"People just got up one day and never came back," Patience says. "Left everything behind, even dirty dishes on the table, clothes hanging on hooks."

"I won't go up there," says Minnie stubbornly. "Remember what you said, Eddie?"

"About the ghost cabin?" Eddie says. "Some fellow died up there and nobody knows how. The cabin's haunted. 'Course, our camp's far away from Sowbelly. There's nothing to worry about."

Even so, I feel nervous as we begin climbing the hill, picking berries as we go. Eddie says he'll show us Sowbelly even though there's hardly anything left of the place. The sides of the gulch are gophered with prospectors' holes, mostly shallow with little mounds of dirt beside them. Sometimes we find a deeper hole and piles of quartz in heaps.

"See the gold?" says Eddie. He picks up a fist-size piece of quartz and licks it so the yellow sparkles through. "That's how the old fellows check for gold."

We're so busy hunting down our own gold, we forget about raspberries and abandon our buckets along the way. It isn't long before we discover a clearing that's inhabited by half a dozen squat log cabins with caved-in roofs and open doors. I peer inside one. Everything has been taken out of the cabin except bedsprings, a bunk, a table, and a broken chair. I push aside a box and find an old shoe, a rusty shovel, and a bent fork.

"Put those b-b-back," Pheme says to me in a low voice.

I do as Pheme asks, not because I'm feeling particularly honest but because I'm thinking of Pa. At this very moment, what kind of poor forsaken mining camp is he living in?

"Look over here!" Eddie calls. We run to the cabin with the closed door. Eddie jerks the latch string and pushes open the door. Something scurries past in the darkness, sounding like a rat. Then the room is silent once again.

*"Heeeee-hawwwww!"*

I jump. Patience screams. Eddie rolls on the ground, laughing. A bony burro pokes his head around the corner of the cabin. He pushes against our pockets for something to eat.

"The mayor of Sowbelly come to welcome us!" Eddie hoots.

"We better get back to camp," I say, frowning at Eddie's joke. "Look at the sky. It's getting dark. Pretty soon we won't be able to find our way."

"We can't leave till we find the berry buckets," Patience says.

It takes us a long time to search for the buckets we left in our search for gold. We only find three. In the distance menacing gray clouds prowl the sky. The wind shifts. I wish I'd brought more warm clothing, because it's going to be a cold night. We start back for camp with the burro following behind us like a dog.

Pheme nudges me with his elbow. He doesn't need to. I can see the flicker of lightning. Thunder rumbles down into the bottoms of our feet. We hurry. Luckily, Folly has not escaped, but he paws the ground nervously. We load more wood on the fire.

"Good thing we've got this tent set up," says Eddie. He crawls under the canvas and takes off his shoes and socks, which he says he intends to use as his pillow. We all climb under the canvas. As soon as we do, the wind begins to lift and billow our tent so violently, we grip the edges tight to keep the whole thing from flying away. Our campfire sputters. Rain drips through the canvas tarp holes. I wish we'd thought to dig a trench around our campsite to help the water run off. A lake forms around our feet.

"I'm cold," says Minnie. "I want to go home."

Thunder booms. There's another tremendous flash of lightning and I sit breathlessly waiting for the next terrible crash. I'm on my knees holding down the end of the sheet. When I turn I see Patience on her hands and knees praying.

"Oh, God, stop the thunder!" she says.

But the wind keeps blowing. "Where's Folly?" Eddie shouts.

I poke my head out from under our flapping canvas. The horse is gone. What will Mr. Cairns say? "Somebody better go out there and try to catch him," I reply, hoping that somebody won't be me.

Nobody volunteers.

"You go, Hattie," Eddie says. "I've got to stay here and help Pheme hold down the tent."

Miserably, I crawl out into the rain and start up the hill. If it weren't for Mr. Cairns's kindness to me, I never would be acting so responsible about his fool horse. Something brown flashes ahead of me among the deadfall of trees. I hear a whinny. "Folly!" I cry. "Come back here." But Folly has other ideas. He must have broken the hobble's leather strap. He's moving up the hill, farther and farther away from camp as if he has no good sense at all.

I stumble along. My dress is damp clear through and my hair is wet. I'm just about to turn back after walking what seems like hours, when I hear another terrible crash and I know there's more rain coming. Somehow I stumble back into Sowbelly. I figure I can crawl into one of the cabins for a while to keep dry.

Shivering, I run across the clearing just as another burst of lightning flashes. I push the door of the nearest cabin. The musty cabin smells like mouse fur and mouse droppings. Rain hammers against the roof and drips inside in one corner where the roof's caved in. I huddle near the doorway, hoping that I haven't picked the cabin Eddie said was haunted. My teeth chatter.

I sit down and try to feel brave. It's drier and warmer

in here than under that old piece of canvas. At least I don't have to listen to Minnie complain. Minutes tick by. I reach in my pocket and find the sulfur-tipped matches in the shell cartridge. I light one and peer around the shadow-filled room. No ghosts. I gather a few pieces of broken chair and part of an old mattress to make a small fire to take away the dampness. How long can the storm last? I wonder.

Once the fire is flickering, I don't feel so frightened. I sit down beside a stack of yellowed, torn newspapers. I tear off a few pages and feed the fire. Inside one copy of *The Middle Park Prospector* I discover a crumpled sheet that looks like part of a letter. I read:

> . . . believe I've struck it rich at last. There was a rush up here three months ago, and I came in soon as the news reached Cheyenne. Must have been several hundred to get here first. No one will work for wages. Everyone is raving crazy, bound to strike it rich, working double shift to hold as many claims as possible. . . .

I think of Pa again and I have a sad pang in my heart. The cabin roof creaks. What's that scratching against the wall? I prop the door open to make myself feel safer, and curl up on the dirt floor beside the fire. I'm so tired after the long climb, I tell myself I'll just shut my eyes for a minute. Suddenly, I'm wide awake. The fire's nearly burned out. It's still raining. I have a strange feeling that there's something or someone else in the room with me. Maybe Eddie was right. Maybe there *is* a ghost.

I gulp and throw a wad of newspaper on the fire and try to go back to sleep. Something thuds close to my head. I open my eyes but lie still, too afraid to move. There's nothing here with me. Nothing, I try to convince myself. Hot breath strikes my face. I jump up and dash for the door. A bulky shadow blocks my way.

Too panicked to scream, I fumble along the wall in the other direction. I'll make my escape out the window. A faint sound comes from that way, too. I back up and decide to run out the door. It slams shut. I scream. Lunging for what I hope is the door latch, I fling open the door and crash into the shape again.

"Heeeee-hawwww!"

The hungry burro takes a few steps forward and noses about my empty pockets.

"Hello, ghost," I say with a relieved laugh. It takes several minutes for my heart to stop beating so wildly. I give the burro a pat and together we hurry down the hill, back to camp.

## TEN

The storm ends. Pheme looks glad to see me when I stumble into camp later that evening. Wet and bedraggled, we spend a chilly night huddled around the smoky fire. In the morning everything looks better. The sun comes up slowly and we manage to find the buckets of berries. Our bread is soggy, but the burro doesn't seem to care. He eats every last crumb. We decide to go home for breakfast. To our surprise, muddy, confused Folly appears between the trees. We saddle him up and hike back down to Lone Squaw.

"You really saw the ghost?" Eddie asks me for the hundredth time.

"Sure," I say, and I wink secretly at Pheme.

Eddie whistles as if he's impressed by my bravery.

Cousin Tirzah doesn't seem happy to see us home so soon. There's no sign of Pug Ryan. Maybe he never came and that's another reason she's in such an evil humor. "This all the raspberries you found?" she asks.

"We got caught in a terrible lightning storm," I say.

Cousin Tirzah acts upset we lost so many buckets, but she seems pleased to have a free burro. That is, until the burro begins eating sheets hanging on the line. "Take him to Old Judge," she tells me. "Maybe he'll want him. He takes in all kinds of other abandoned animals."

I'm delighted to have the opportunity to visit Old Judge and maybe have a hot meal. When I give a two-barreled whistle to my brother, he doesn't answer. Off I trot with the burro, who follows me willingly as long as I offer him scraps of rancid hog rind. I'm so hungry, my stomach feels as if it's sticking to my backbone.

"Hello, Sinner," Old Judge says when he sees me. "Looking for your brother? He's already gone hunting. Lent him one of my guns."

"Pheme went hunting? He's never gone by himself before. You think he'll be all right?"

"He'll be fine. Who's your friend?"

"A burro who found us up near Sowbelly where we were looking for raspberries. Cousin Tirzah says she wants to give him to you because he eats laundry." I sniff. I can smell something good cooking.

Old Judge inspects the burro. "His ribs stick out like a washboard's. So do yours. Let's give this fellow some feed and see about some grub for you."

Old Judge pours some oats into a bag, and the burro eats so fast I'm sure he'll get sick. As soon as he finishes the last bit, he trots away. "Lot of these burros aren't so lucky. When miners pull up stakes, they leave the extra burros to starve," says Old Judge. He opens the cabin door for me like a real gentleman.

I'm surprised to see one of Pheme's sketches on the table. It's a mountain scene I recognize from our trip above the timberline. "Pheme give you this?" I ask. I can't help feeling a little jealous. Why didn't Pheme show me first?

"He made my portrait, too," Old Judge says proudly. "The likeness was so good, it spooked Sinbad. Of course, dogs aren't reliable art critics."

I can't keep from laughing. Old Judge sets a coffeepot to boil on a hook inside the big fireplace. He pokes potatoes with their jackets on, deep in the coals, and arranges two fat trout in a pan.

I sit down at the table. "Pheme doesn't show his sketches to many people. He hasn't sketched in such a long time, I thought maybe he gave up for good."

"Your brother has real artistic talent. It would be a shame if he stopped sketching. All he needs is encouragement."

Encouragement. I like that word.

Old Judge checks the potatoes and flips the sputtering fish in the pan. As I watch him work, I think about the way people warned me about him. They were wrong. So was I. Old Judge isn't a mean old coot. Anybody who can encourage my brother to talk and laugh and sketch again is pretty remarkable, as far as I'm concerned.

But what does Old Judge think of me? Am I worth encouraging? Sometimes I brag. Sometimes I eavesdrop. Sometimes I lie. Sometimes I fight. I'm not artistic. I can't recite poems from memory or shoot a gun like Pheme. Come to think of it, I don't have much in the way of talent. Even so, I long to know how I measure up in Old Judge's eyes.

"Something on your mind, Sinner?" Old Judge asks.

"Cousin Tirzah once called me a little, pitiful, despicable worm. Do I seem as wretched and awful as all that?"

Old Judge gives the fire a poke. "Most certainly not," he says in a serious voice. "If I thought so, would I have invited you in for a bite to eat?"

I shrug. "Why *did* you invite me?"

"I invited you because I enjoy your company, Sinner. Something about you reminds me of myself. Once upon a time I was just as feisty as you. Not for one minute was I willing to accept the unfair predicament I found myself in. Hard-eyed, that's what they called me. But I was just plain stubborn. I had plans for my future that my family just couldn't seem to understand."

I try to imagine Old Judge when he was ten years old and feisty. Try as I might, I can't make him look any younger. In my mind he remains just as gray and grizzled as he is now, only he's shorter.

"Another reason I enjoy your company, Sinner, is you never ask humiliating questions. Most folks could learn a lot from your example."

I'm so pleased that when the fish and potatoes are ready, I eat three enormous helpings—more than I'd ever be allowed at Cousin Tirzah's. As a special surprise, Old Judge gives me a chunk of sweet cake with currants that he baked himself. Old Judge's food tastes better than anything I ever ate in all my days. I don't think he believes me, but he looks proud when I tell him. He sets out his old checkerboard.

"I'm a fierce checkers player, Sinner," he warns. "But I'll show you all the tricks I know."

I soon realize I had better be more careful. Old Judge does not like to lose.

"You're sure nobody ever played checkers with you before?" Old Judge asks, his eyes narrowing. This is our fifth game. I've beaten him three times already.

"Yes, sir."

"Well, I'll have to admit, you certainly learn quickly. You're a clever girl."

I smile. People call me all sorts of things. Nobody ever calls me clever.

Old Judge lights his pipe. I'm glad Pheme's not here. I'm glad I have Old Judge to myself for once. The best thing about being alone with Old Judge is the talking. That's what I enjoy. Old Judge forgets I'm only ten years old and treats me like I'm a real person.

I enjoy the Greek myths and the stories from *The Arabian Nights* he tells while we play checkers. But best of all, I enjoy hearing him talk about Lone Squaw in the early days, when there was no one here except him. Most Indians stayed away because they believed the lake was haunted.

"Sometimes I think they're right about the lake's bad spirits. Take the first winter I came here, for example. I nearly starved to death," he says, watching pipe smoke float. "There was this young fellow, a trapper, who stumbled into my camp one day before the first snow fell. He seemed like an agreeable sort. I trusted him. So when he said he'd take my large catch of trout across the range to Georgetown, sell them, and return with a winter's supply of food, I believed him."

"What happened then?"

"I waited. A few weeks passed. The weather was still

tolerably warm, so I thought to myself, He'll be back any day. Then the big freeze came. The temperature dropped, the lake went solid. The wind blew. The snow drifted right over my chimney. It was a terrible winter."

"Did he come back?"

"No, he did not. I knew I'd have to spend the rest of the winter with the few supplies I had left and what I could trap or catch for myself to eat. There was less than a hundred pounds of flour in the cabin. I cut holes in the ice to fish, but the trout stopped biting. I snared a few rabbits, but after a while, the heavy snow even discouraged them. I'll tell you, I was hungry."

"What did you do?"

"I took a deerskin hide from my wall, scraped it, cut the hide in pieces, and boiled it in melted snow water. It was a kind of soup. Tasted like glue, but it was better than nothing. When that was nearly gone, I decided I was finished. I was too weak to get out of bed. Then one day two beaver trappers found me. They had come over the pass and were looking for a place to stay. They saw my cabin, no smoke coming from the chimney, and decided to investigate. If it hadn't been for them, I'd be dead."

"Then what happened?"

"There's not much more to tell. Here I am," Old Judge says, and laughs.

"What happened to the two trappers?"

"They stayed a month or more. Restocked my supplies with fresh game. Soon it was spring again; the ice melted, and I could fish. They went on their way."

"Were they your friends?"

Old Judge ponders this question a long time. "I never

saw them again. I suppose they were wanderers, too. Just like me."

"Wanderers?"

"I used to do a lot of moving around—that was after I escaped from Connecticut. You see, my father wanted me to be a lawyer. I tried that for a while. But I could never measure up to my family's grand expectations. So I ran away."

"What did you do then?"

"Traveled around the country, working as a farmhand, a cook, a livery man. All kinds of odd jobs. I tried herding sheep. I even tried acting with a traveling theater company. Then I joined the Union Army for a while. The war ended. My health failed. I decided to try my luck in Colorado, regain my strength, maybe find a fortune in gold."

"Did you ever go back and see your family again?"

"No, I did not," Old Judge says slowly. "I suppose I was afraid I'd disappointed them too much. My parents passed away years ago. It's too late to try and heal old wounds." Old Judge stares off into space. "Funny thing, I don't remember anymore what I left home looking for."

Absentmindedly, I stare at my black checker pieces. One does not match. I pick up and examine the rough, unpainted, knuckle-sized chunk of pine. I think of Old Judge. He doesn't match either. He's not like anyone I ever met before. But I think he's fine, just the way he is. I make my move. "King me," I say.

"You won again, Sinner. You're a mean checker player, you know that?"

I smile. "That's right, Saint J.L. When my pa gets here, I'll show him how I play. I want him to see everything I've learned, how to cast and how to troll and how to hunt fat grasshoppers for trout bait and how to make sweet currant cake without milk or eggs and how to tie a fishing fly so it looks like a mayfly with a beard. I bet you'll like Pa. Just wait."

"All right, Sinner," Old Judge replies. He dumps the checkers into a box.

"You think my pa's coming back, don't you?" I ask anxiously. What if Old Judge is just trying to humor me?

"Why sure," Old Judge says. "Why shouldn't your pa come back?"

I don't reply. What if Pa is wandering, just like Old Judge did long ago? What if Pheme and I never see Pa again, just like Old Judge's family never again saw him?

I'm not sure why, but I'm crying. I'm sobbing real loud. It's as if the worry and the waiting and the sorrow has come crashing down on me at once. I miss Pa. And I miss Mama worst of all.

"Here, take this," Old Judge says, handing me a big red handkerchief to blow my nose and wipe the tears streaming down my face. "Go ahead and have a good cry."

I tell Old Judge my whole, sad story. I tell him how lost and miserable I felt when Mama died and Pa left us. I tell him how we've waited and waited and still Pa hasn't written to us to tell us where he is or when he is coming to get us. "I hate Cousin Tirzah," I say in a trembling voice. "I hate living with her and Patience and Eddie and Minnie. They're mean and horrible. You know, you're the first person who's really listened to me and Pheme since we came here."

"There, there now, Sinner. Everything will be all right," Old Judge says in a soothing voice.

I blow my nose again. I'm surprised how easily I told

Old Judge about what has happened to me and Pheme. I'm surprised I told Old Judge the whole story without once lying or changing the truth.

"You feel better now?" Old Judge asks.

I nod and take a deep breath. Yes, I do feel better.

## ELEVEN

Today is the Fourth of July, the biggest celebration of the year in Last Chance. Hundreds of miners come into town from all over the mountains, Eddie says. They come to watch the horse races and the tug-of-war matches and the wrestling contests. They shoot off their guns and blast firecrackers and raise a regular hullabaloo. Secretly, I'm hoping today we'll hear from Pa. And why not? With so many miners in town, there must be one from up the Neversummer way. Maybe Pa sent along a message with somebody for us. Maybe there's a hand-delivered letter just waiting for me and Pheme at Mr. Cairns's store.

While Pheme and I roll up our bedding, Cousin Tirzah stomps into the room. "Nobody can leave the cabin today," she announces. "You children have to stay indoors, where you'll be safe."

"Why?" I ask, disappointed.

"The Fourth of July in Last Chance is one Devil-made

tangle-brain. That is all I am going to say, Harriet Elizabeth Proctor. There is sinful drinking and sinful dancing and sinful cardplaying and sinful swearing and shooting and fighting when those hard-rock scrabblers and miners come down from the hills. I will not have you or your brother or any of my children around such heathen and immoral behavior. You will stay inside and you will pray."

"Ma'am, just like Sabbath?" I say in disbelief.

"Just like Sabbath," Cousin Tirzah replies sternly.

Commissioner John G. Mills, whose grave is marked in the Last Chance cemetery, was shot on the Fourth of July. On the Fourth of July, guns blast. Horses stampede. Women faint. I don't want to miss the excitement. And if we're trapped indoors, how will Pheme and I sneak away to town to check for Pa's letter? It isn't fair. I sigh loudly.

Cousin Tirzah ignores me. Lord Calvert is waiting for breakfast. She slams the boards on top of the sawhorses and flips the oilcloth in place.

"Madam, it is my duty as a gentleman to offer my servant's services. Samuel will stand guard outside the cabin," Lord Calvert announces from the doorway, sweeping off his new cowboy hat. "It's going to be one hell-roaring jamboree, as they say in this country. Samuel will prevent any tanked-up celebrant from annoying you and your family."

Samuel, who stands behind Lord Calvert, raises one finger to the rim of his hat. He does not smile.

"That's right kind of you. Now sit down and make yourself comfortable, Lord Calvert. I'll have your trout fried in no time," Cousin Tirzah says. She chops off a fish head and throws it into a gut bucket.

After Lord Calvert is finished eating and has politely

excused himself, me and Pheme and the rest of the children sit down for morning prayers. Fast as we can, we gobble our portions of boiled cornmeal. Patience and I go to work on the dishes. When we're done, Cousin Tirzah tells me to keep careful watch of Willie while she cleans the guest cabin. Willie, Pheme, and I sit at one end of the room on the floor. Eddie sits on the other. Patience and Minnie are at the table looking at the colored pictures in Cousin Tirzah's enormous ten-dollar Bible.

Eddie takes out his jackknife and wipes the blade on the seat of his pants. "This is the same kind of knife that marked the spot where they hid the gold."

I look up, suddenly interested. "What are you talking about?"

"Long time ago seven men dug up some gold in California. They came east when Utes jumped them over near Steamboat Springs. Well, three died, but four got away with the gold dust. Made it all the way to Lone Squaw Lake. Then they camped and rested and fished for a few days."

"Then what happened?" I demand.

"The prospectors said, 'These bags of gold are slowing us down. We gotta move fast across the Plains or lose our scalps.' So they dumped the gold dust in a big Dutch oven and buried it next to a boulder on the east shore. Just to make sure they'd find the gold when they came back, one of the fellows stuck his hunting knife in the trunk of a pine tree close by."

"Tell her about the murders. The scalpings!" Minnie exclaims, and smacks her hands together. Willie claps his hands, too, even though he doesn't know what all his sister's fuss is about.

"The prospectors tangled with Indians. Three more of 'em got killed," says Eddie. "Only one made it home. He came into Missouri, told his story about the Dutch oven to a friend, and one day fell over dead."

"All that work for nothing," Patience says, and sniffs.

"Did anyone ever find the gold?" I ask, sitting Willie in my lap.

Patience and Minnie shake their heads. "Lots of people have tried," Eddie says. "Nobody's ever found it."

Looking for gold somebody has already found sounds a far sight easier than prospecting from scratch. "Why don't we look for that knife?" I ask eagerly.

"I bet we can find the gold dust," Eddie says.

Pheme frowns and shakes his head.

"What's the matter? Don't you believe my story, dogie?" Eddie demands.

Pheme doesn't answer, but I can tell he's insulted by the name Eddie calls him.

"How about if we sing a song?" I suggest quickly.

"Better sing a church song this time," Patience warns. "Ma doesn't like any other kind."

Willie leans against my shoulder. I take a deep breath and sing the first note of the first hymn that comes into my head—"Sweet Hour of Prayer." When I finish I'm pleased that Patience and Minnie are clapping.

"I liked the di-a-ree song better," Eddie grumbles.

"Pheme knows more verses than I do, don't you, Pheme?" I say.

My brother refuses to answer. He wipes his eyes with his shirtsleeve and I wonder what's wrong with him. While the others are busy jumping on the bed, I ask Pheme, "What's the matter?"

"Don't s-s-s-sing that s-s-s-song again."

"Why?" I demand. I thought I did a good job, remembering as many verses as I had. What was wrong with my song?

"Just don't s-s-s-sing it."

I put Willie under the table to play with clothespins. To make time go faster, I help Patience with mending, even though my stitching's anything but neat. As I work, the words from the hymn keep repeating in my head.

> *In seasons of distress and grief,*
> *My soul has often found relief,*
> *And oft escaped the tempter's snare*
> *By thy return, sweet hour of prayer.*

Then I remember. Mama sang that melody. She taught me the words when I was barely big enough to climb up on her high bed. Long, long ago, when she still had good days, she'd gently brush my hair and sing old hymns. "Sweet Hour of Prayer" was one of her favorites. Pheme knew that, too.

I smile. It doesn't make me sad or angry to remember the song. It makes me happy. I am remembering something warm and tender about Mama, a memory I pushed away and hid for so long.

Suddenly we hear the sound of gunshots. Patience jumps. Willie grabs my leg.

"You know what they do down by the lake?" says Eddie eagerly. He flips the jackknife against the wall.

"What?" I ask nervously. I sit on the floor and draw Willie up in my lap again.

Eddie is playing mumblety-peg on the dirt floor, seeing how far he can throw without stabbing somebody. His knife whizzes and bites the ground, a few inches from me and Willie. Nervously, I tuck my feet under myself. Eddie leans over and picks up his knife. He moves to the other side of the room again.

"On the Fourth of July, they set up a big tent with a wood dance floor," Eddie says. Zip! The knife narrowly misses Pheme's foot.

"There's a fiddler who comes from Teller," Eddie continues, "and everyone plays cards and dances all night. Then there's a footrace and a rock-drilling contest and lots of fights."

Eddie throws. Pheme moves his hand, just in time. Eddie smiles as he picks up the knife.

"S-s-stop it!" Pheme says in a low, menacing voice.

"Can't understand a word you're blubbering," Eddie replies. He rubs the sharp blade. Then he sends it flying. I can feel the knife bite the air as it whirls past my arm and Willie's head.

Pheme jumps to his feet. He reaches in his pocket and pulls out the jackknife Pa gave him. "D-d-don't throw anymore."

"Will if I want to." Eddie sneers and flings his knife, which lands just inches from Pheme's foot. In a flash, Pheme charges across the room and butts Eddie in the stomach with his head. Eddie crashes onto his back, arms swinging, as Pheme straddles his chest. Pheme, his eyes flashing, his face flushed, holds his knife over Eddie's neck. Eddie lies trembling.

"Patience! Throw me my knife!" Eddie pleads.

Patience does not respond. She just stands there with a dull expression, watching to see what will happen next. Willie buries his face in my apron.

"You going to kill him?" Minnie asks curiously. No one volunteers to get Cousin Tirzah. Maybe Minnie and her sister don't care what happens to Eddie.

Two big tears roll out of Eddie's eyes. "Don't stab me. Please don't stab me. I'll never say nothing if you'll just let me go."

Pheme seems to be considering. After a few moments, he puts his knife back in his pocket and crawls off Eddie. Eddie wipes his nose with the back of his arm. He doesn't look one bit like a tough vigilante as he staggers to his feet and slumps into a chair.

"That's all you're going to do?" Minnie asks, disappointed.

Pheme nods. "L-l-let's go, Hattie," he says. "We're missing the F-F-Fourth of July."

"All right!" I reply, amazed and delighted by Pheme's boldness. I hand Willie to Patience. I can hardly wait to go into Last Chance and see the fancy hurdy-gurdy girls all dressed up with feathers and jewels and such. "But what about Eddie and Minnie and Patience? They'll tell Cousin Tirzah where we've gone."

Pheme gives Eddie a threatening look.

"We'll keep quiet," Eddie mumbles.

I poke my head out the doorway. Samuel has his chair tipped back against the cabin wall. He takes a swig from a jug of Taos Lightning and hides it again in a fish crate. I motion to Pheme and point to two buckets.

"Samuel," I say, "my brother and I are going to the lake for water."

Samuel's not interested. He nods and waves us past. Pheme and I bolt down the lake path. We hide the buckets in the bushes and hurry to town.

Main Street is noisy and crowded. At Mr. Cairns's store, the door is closed. A sign in the window says: "Gone dancing."

"Maybe he's in the t-t-tent," Pheme suggests. "Want to l-l-look?"

"Sure!" I reply. "You know, Pheme, you handled Eddie just fine. I was real proud of you."

Pheme smiles.

Nobody pays any attention to us when we crawl on all fours and lift a piece of canvas tarp to look inside the tent. The dancing is wild and colorful and, best of all, very wicked. Boots stomp and high-step past to the fiddle music. I count a dozen or more flashing, whirling ladies with ringlets and curly hairdos and ribbons and lace and valuable-looking bracelets and jangling necklaces and rings. Their cheeks glow bright red but otherwise their faces are unnaturally white, like the color of chalk.

I don't spot Mr. Cairns. Miners in their best boiled-wool shirts, denim overalls, and heavy boots dance past with carbide lamps still on their caps. Their faces are as stubbly and scarred as the stump-covered hillsides outside town. The men shout and joke and holler and pound each other on the backs. Everyone's having a wonderful time. I don't hear one grown-up complain about pinched-out placers or choking yellow smelter smoke.

A pair of cowboy boots waltzes by, kicking and clanking, spurs a-jangle. A cowboy with slick, parted hair and a brilliant red bandanna around his neck taps the toe of his boot. He looks like he's itching to dance, but there aren't enough lady partners to go around. Finally, he gives up waiting and dances with another cowboy.

"Swing your partner like swingin' on a gate," bellows the caller, standing on a box. "Swing her again and promenade eight!"

"Come on, Pheme!" I laugh, tugging him to his feet.

Pheme swings me around and around in a patch of dirt outside the tent. I laugh and tumble dizzily into the dust. A cowboy comes teetering around the corner of the tent and decides we're enjoying the music without paying the proper admission of fifty cents. Since we don't have any money, he chases us away. "Get out of here, rascals!"

Pheme and I run breathless and laughing to the other side of the tent, where we hide a while longer, watching the next dance. I am light-headed and happy. I like being a rascal.

Finally I say, "Pheme, if we can't find Mr. Cairns, maybe we better go back to Cousin Tirzah's. I'll race you!" Fiddle music is still rollicking in my head. My feet prance light and graceful along the lake trail. I leap across the stream in three bounds. I have wings! I can fly!

## TWELVE

When Pheme and I sneak around the corner of the cabin, we can hear Cousin Tirzah talking. We tiptoe through the open door. Eddie and the others are standing around the table. They ignore us because they are so busy studying a seated stranger. Fast as he can, the stranger shovels fried salt pork and beans into his mouth with the flat blade of his knife. Cousin Tirzah works at the stove, her back toward the door. I hold my breath and we take another step. Maybe she won't notice us. Maybe she won't holler.

Too late. Cousin Tirzah twirls around. "What do you two think you're doing?" she says angrily. "While you and your halfwit brother were disobeying me, Harriet Elizabeth Proctor, somebody came with a message from your pa." She jerks her head in the direction of the stranger, who keeps eating without bothering to look up.

"Here," Cousin Tirzah says. She hands me a soiled piece of paper with Pa's handwriting.

My dearest children:

I'm not sure when I'll return precisely, but I hope before snow falls. Don't worry about me. May God bless and keep you safe.

Your loving father

Excitedly, I ask the stranger, "Who are you? You saw our pa? How does he look? Is he all right?"

The man wipes his greasy mouth with the back of his hand. He has close-set gray eyes that remind me of a coyote's. "I'm just a messenger. Your pa promised me somebody would pay a good silver piece or two if I'd deliver that note. I ain't saying more till I get paid."

Pheme looks at me, his eyes filled with desperation. "Cousin Tirzah," I ask as sweetly as I can, "will you give him a silver piece? I promise to pay you back. My word's good."

"Already gave the man supper," Cousin Tirzah complains.

"Please!" I beg. "This fellow's the only one who knows where Pa is."

Cousin Tirzah opens her ledger book and pencils a mark. "All right," she growls. She hands me a coin from a small pouch she has hidden inside her apron pocket.

I press the coin into the man's grimy hand. "Now tell us where he is."

"Your pa's up near Rabbit Ears Pass in the Neversummer Range. The placer's just past Hitchens Gulch."

"How do you get there from here?"

The stranger scratches his neck with the tip of his knife. "Follow Columbine Creek east, along the old Indian trail.

Leads up Rabbit Ears Pass. Once you're over the mountain, stay hard on the trail till you cross the North Fork. Hitchens Gulch is up the river to the north, three miles or more."

"Is Pa all right?" I demand. "Does he have enough to eat? He isn't sick, is he?"

"I think I told enough for one silver coin," the messenger says, tucking the money inside his pocket and heading for the door. "And if there ain't no more vittles, I best be moving on."

"What's your name?" I call to him from the doorway. He doesn't answer as he disappears down the hill.

"Can we believe him?" I mumble to my brother. Pheme gives me a bewildered shrug.

"If you want supper, you better sit down," Cousin Tirzah says to us. She thumps bowls and plates on the table. " 'I'll come before the snow.' I've heard that promise before. Well, it's a good thing I've got sense enough to make other plans for you two."

"Other plans?" I ask, shooting a worried glance at Pheme.

"You'll find out soon enough," Cousin Tirzah says between her teeth. "Eddie, go call to Lord Calvert. Supper's ready."

We fight for chairs at the table and bow our heads for prayers. Lord Calvert slips into his chair just as Cousin Tirzah announces, "Amen."

"Amen," Lord Calvert echoes. "Madam, is it elk stew tonight?"

"With your favorite dumplings, too, your lordship," Cousin Tirzah says. She spoons an extra-large helping onto

Lord Calvert's bowl. "Pass this to our *paying* guest, Patience."

Patience does as she's told.

"Lord Calvert, I'd like your opinion," Cousin Tirzah says.

"Certainly," he replies.

"Would you agree that there's nothing preventing a good Christian from being a good businessman?"

"Absolutely, madam!" Lord Calvert says, and lifts the spoon to his mouth. "Although I confess I fail to think of an example at this particular moment."

"Well, I know a good Christian businessman. His name is Mr. Pug Ryan," Cousin Tirzah continues. "He's clever and devout. Mr. Pug Ryan says he needs help up at the Coming Wonder mine near Lulu City. And he knows a woman who runs the Grand Imperial Hotel in Fairplay, with a piano and real fancy furniture. She's looking for someone to help her clean and do laundry. Mr. Pug Ryan says he can make all the arrangements and I'll get the first six months' wages for my trouble. Enough for me to invest in a little real estate."

"That's the energetic, go-ahead American spirit!" Lord Calvert says, thumping down his spoon. "But, madam, I don't see how you can possibly work two more jobs. Fairplay and Lulu City are two days' travel apart."

"The jobs aren't for me, your lordship," Cousin Tirzah replies. And she gazes iron-hard in my direction and then in Pheme's.

I feel gagged for breath. Cousin Tirzah's gray eyes hold fast. The Coming Wonder. The Grand Imperial Hotel. I know all about those horrible places. My palms sweat.

"Eddie, pass the stewed tomatoes after you help your-self," Cousin Tirzah orders. She dumps one small tomato in my bowl and quietly, deliberately announces, "This is a business—not an orphange for every child who wanders over the pass."

*Orphanage.* I don't like that hateful word. I clench my fists in anger but I keep my arms stiff at my sides. Me and Pheme aren't orphans. We still have Pa. We just don't know when he's coming to get us, that's all.

I take a spoonful of brown beans swimming in hominy and turn the beans over and over again. Pheme's face is pale, as if all the life has gone out of him. He hasn't touched his food. I can't blame him. Pug Ryan is going to send him to the bottom of the dangerous, dirty, flooded Coming Won-der. A hellhole, that's what that boy with the missing fingers called it. And he considered himself lucky just to get out alive.

What about me? Lonely and forgotten. Washing floors and windows at the Grand Imperial Hotel for the rest of my life. Just like poor Lulita.

"Would you like some more dumplings, Lord Calvert?" Cousin Tirzah asks.

"Thank you, I don't mind if I do," Lord Calvert says. "It's amazing how this altitude makes one hungry! Why, the other day I was just saying to Samuel how healthful this climate is. You are so fortunate to live here year-round and enjoy the benefits of it every day."

Cousin Tirzah ladles three more wet gray dumplings on her own plate. "Some winter try feeding seven on what's meant for only five," she grumbles.

"In this region there are bears larger, stronger, and

more difficult to kill than any lions I encountered in Algiers. Hunting bear is my passion. It's a sport," Lord Calvert says, pausing dramatically, "for those who settle little value upon life. I hope to take an excellent trophy home with me before snow closes the pass. The Monarch of the Mountain is what I seek."

"Monarch?" Cousin Tirzah says, and snorts. "No such thing up here."

"*Ursus horribilis,* my good woman." Lord Calvert laughs and daintily dabs his mustache with his linen handkerchief. The hanky has pretty initials sewn on one corner. "I found a magnificent beast's pawprint pressed into the mud near Rabbit Ears Pass. Nearly twelve inches long, not including claws. Quite a grizzly bear specimen. Perhaps a thousand pounds. I'd estimate he's nine feet tall, standing on his legs."

My brother looks up from his bowl of beans for the first time.

"Bears is bears. Last spring one killed all my pigs I was counting on for bacon and ham," Cousin Tirzah replies. She orders Patience to gather empty plates and bowls as soon as Lord Calvert excuses himself and leaves the cabin. "Patience and Minnie, get some fresh water to wash the dishes. Harriet, you and that brother of yours can go and get more firewood."

Eddie smiles nastily. Filling the wood box is usually his job. "Tough luck!" Eddie says under his breath, and follows Pheme outside.

There's no one left inside the cabin except me and Cousin Tirzah. Cousin Tirzah is usually first on her feet when a meal is finished, but this evening she remains at the table, her shoulders slightly slumped forward, staring at a worn spot in the oilcloth. I try to tiptoe past without her noticing, but she calls to me before I can escape. "Girl," she says, "when I was your age I earned my living. My pa sent me away to work in that button factory. That was how I was raised up."

I suck in my breath as if I'd just been dunked in cold water. Cousin Tirzah's never told me this part of the story before. "Your *pa* sent you away?"

Cousin Tirzah does not look up. "There were thirteen of us. We was starving. He didn't have no choice. I had to go."

I'm thinking she'll tell me how being sent away by her pa didn't bother her none. I expect to hear her explain how working in that button factory was "toil and privation and pain" that made her a better Christian.

But Cousin Tirzah doesn't speak of any of those things. I don't know why, but suddenly I can imagine Cousin Tirzah in a way I never thought of before. She's a hurting, hopeless ten-year-old, just like me.

"Cousin Tirzah . . ." I say softly, thinking maybe now we can understand each other. Maybe now I can argue her out of selling me and Pheme.

I am mistaken.

"I warned you this would happen. You wouldn't listen," Cousin Tirzah says, and briskly pushes back her chair. She stands up and looks at me coolly. I can see that her mind is made up. "Mr. Pug Ryan is a patient, God-fearing man, but he won't bide his time forever. A deal is a deal. I'm letting him know tomorrow that he can take you and your brother off my hands, once and for all."

"But Cousin Tirzah, what happens if Pa gets here and we're gone?" I ask, my voice rising with panic.

"It's God's will," she whispers, her hot breath rushing past my cheek like the wind of the four angels in the four corners of heaven. "I've waited long enough. Your pa isn't ever coming back."

In town, shouting and shooting and singing echo through the night. I lie on the floor, wrapped in Cousin Tirzah's comforter, confused and frightened. I worry about what is to become of me and Pheme. I worry about Pa. Over and over again, I try to remember exactly what the stranger said. Was it up Columbine Creek to the Indian trail that leads to Rabbit Ears Pass? That makes sense. Pheme and I have hiked that way before. It's the part about the North Fork I can't remember exactly.

"Pheme, you awake?" I call to the lump on the cot. As soon as I hear him roll over, I whisper all I know about the Fairplay Hotel and the Coming Wonder Mine. I got to prove to him just how much danger we're facing. But when I finish, Pheme doesn't say anything. Not even a grunt.

I sigh, wondering if Pheme's just pretending to be asleep. "Pheme, talk to me! Did that man say north along the river to Hitchens Gulch? I've got to know for sure, because I'm going to go look for Pa."

"It's too d-d-dangerous for you, Hattie. B-b-besides, we're not sure where P-P-Pa is," Pheme replies quietly. "Go to sleep."

I close my eyes, but sleep won't come. I keep thinking about Pa. I can see him so clearly. He's on his way to save us from Pug Ryan, I'm sure. Why, any moment he'll be at Cousin Tirzah's door. He'll be hungry from his long walk. I have to get things ready. I have to get him something to eat.

Quietly, I crawl out of the comforter and slip three sticks of wood into the stove. I fill the coffeepot with a dipper of water from the pail. In the darkness I fumble for the loaf of bread I know is wrapped in a flour-sack towel and tucked inside the tin pie safe.

Just as I open the wooden door and put my hand on the loaf, I hear something. It's a sorrowful cry coming from outside. "Pa?" I call, my voice trembling.

"Now what are you d-d-doing?" Pheme complains.

"I'm . . . I'm fixing something for Pa. He's coming. I know he's coming."

Something outside, something we can't see, is crying again.

"Did you hear that?" I whisper.

"It's just that b-b-burro looking for food. Hattie, go to s-s-sleep." Pheme angrily turns over and pulls his blanket over his head.

I am sitting up, listening. That poor, deserted burro. Pheme and I, aren't we just like him? "Pheme!" I whisper frantically. "What if something horrible happened to Pa? What if that stranger took his gold and hurt him? What if he's got the fever and he's sick and dying?"

Pheme pretends to be sound asleep so I'll finally shut up. I lean back and peer out one of the open chinks in the log wall. The cold, clear night sky is crowded with winking stars. They are no comfort to me. I am as lonely and forgotten as I have ever felt in my whole life.

# THIRTEEN

Someone roughly shakes me awake. It's Cousin Tirzah. "Where's your brother? Where did he go?"

Outside I hear the yells and curses of a grown man, a crazy grown man. A gun blasts. I pull the blanket over my face and hide. "Who's making all that noise?" I mumble, confused and still half asleep.

"That no-good Old Judge. He's having his drinking spree and there will be the Devil to pay. He nearly shot a hole through Mr. Pug Ryan earlier this morning. Luckily, Mr. Ryan managed to escape unharmed. He'll be back, though, you can be sure."

I leap to my feet, nearly dizzy with happiness. Mr. Pug Ryan scared away! I feel as if I've been spared. But as I look around the room, at Pheme's empty bed and the frightened faces of Cousin Tirzah's children, I realize something terrible has happened. I listen hard. And suddenly the idea that Old

Judge might have changed and become loud and crazy and violent gives me the chills.

"Where's Pheme?" I demand.

"That's what I'm asking *you*. I reckon he left last night. What do you know about it?" Cousin Tirzah replies angrily. "And you better tell me before Mr. Ryan comes back again."

I scramble across the room and open the flap covering the window.

"What do you think you're doing? Get away from that window!" Cousin Tirzah snaps the canvas shut. "You want that poisonous old varmint to put a bullet through your head?"

"I have to find my brother. What if he's hurt?"

"Well, you won't find him by staring outside like that," she says. She shuffles to the stove and raps a wooden spoon against a large pan of bubbling porridge. Then Cousin Tirzah stands perfectly still. She's listening to the noises outside, I can tell. Is she afraid, too? "Old Judge is tanked up drunker than a dog on Taos Lightning. Does this every year." She hands me a stack of bowls to put around the table. "When he gets drunk like this, he's mean as the very Devil. May the good Lord preserve us. The only thing to do is stay far away and hope nobody gets hurt."

"What about Old Judge? What if he shoots himself? Can't anybody stop him?" I ask.

"No one excepting a fool," she says darkly. "He's best left alone till the liquor's gone and he works himself out of it. In my mind, wouldn't be so much of a loss if he put an end to his miserable self. That man's a menace. And to think

I had hopes he was reformed, the way he shared his fish so neighborly and all. I guess I was wrong."

All through breakfast I try to think. I need a plan. I'm worried about Old Judge, so wild and mean. He might hurt himself or somebody else. How could he have changed into a person I no longer know and maybe no longer trust? It seems crazy, impossible. But I can't desert him. What should I do? While I want to help Old Judge, I know I must search for Pheme. It isn't like him to run away like this without telling me where he's going or when he'll be back.

Cousin Tirzah's children are unusually quiet as they eat hot porridge. I hold Willie on my lap because he is so fretful. Patience squints toward the window every now and again.

A brief knock startles us. I pray it's Pheme. Nobody moves. Cousin Tirzah peeks out the window before she unbars the door. Standing pale and shaken in the doorway is Samuel. He comes inside and lowers himself onto a chair.

"Humph! Look at what the cat dragged in!" Cousin Tirzah announces, her hands on her hips. "Wait until Lord Calvert finds out how you disobeyed him last night. Wait till he hears how you disappeared over to that sinful dance hall."

"Sorry, ma'am," Samuel says, and winces as if her piercing voice hurts his ears. "Say, ma'am, could you spare a cup of strong coffee? My head throbs awful."

Cousin Tirzah hands Samuel a mug. He sips slowly, unaware how closely he is being watched by each of us around the table. "That old fellow out there is loading every gun he owns," Samuel says in a low voice, as if only Cousin Tirzah can hear. "The old buzzard would have murdered me if I hadn't slunk low behind the trees. He's sitting on the footbridge, threatening to shoot anybody who tries to enter Hell's Gate. Something about how he won't let young souls be sold to slavery. Lincoln freed the slaves, didn't he? Now what do you suppose he means?"

"He's just talking gibberish. Drunken Union soldier gibberish," Cousin Tirzah replies with disgust. "Now tell me. When you were in town earlier this morning, did you hear anything? Did anyone volunteer to go to Old Judge's and take his guns away?"

Samuel mops his brow with his handkerchief. "Absolutely not. The old man is not only crazy, they say he was once a dead shot."

"That was years ago!" Cousin Tirzah exclaims. "The way he sees, he probably couldn't hit the broad side of a barn three paces away."

I help Patience clear the dishes from the table. Slowly, I dunk the bowls into a pail of water and rub them clean. I know what I have to do. I must go to Old Judge's house and try to talk sense into him. Maybe I can calm him down and convince him to put away his guns. I have to try. I can't abandon Old Judge the way everyone else has.

"Ma, do we have to stay inside again all day?" Eddie complains.

"That's right. As long as Old Judge is drunk, you'll stay here where you're safe," Cousin Tirzah replies. "There's plenty to be done. I'm going out to fetch a pail of clean water. You can all help me clean and scrub."

As soon as Cousin Tirzah disappears for water, I jump out the window. I land on my hands and knees, get up, and run so fast the forest on either side of me seems only a green blur.

I balance across the footbridge, scoot behind a tree, and wait. From inside his cabin I can hear Old Judge hollering and cussing, fit to bust. He comes outside carrying every gun he owns. He's talking to himself and his speech is slurred and crazy. His hat is gone. I've never seen him hatless before. His forehead is pale compared to the rest of his weathered, tanned face. His grizzled hair stands straight up on the top of his head. Clumsily, he rams powder and shot.

"Here's Old Jezebel," Old Judge announces, picking up a double-barreled muzzle-loading shotgun, five feet long. "If ye can pack her, he sure can kill anything that wears hair. She eats nails, slugs, and bolts. Right 'ere's Old Henry. He only shoots on rainy days an' Sundays. That pizen old reptile thar killed the feller that invented it."

"Hello, Saint J.L.," I call loud and clear. Taking a deep breath, I step out from my hiding place.

"Sinner, you seen Old Satan? Can't find him anywhere. You know the gun I mean. Stands six feet in his shimmy an' he drops steel yards at ten pounds. He's good for half a mile backwards and forwards, mostly back."

"What are you doing with all these guns, Saint J.L.? I thought we were going fishing today."

Old Judge looks at me, struggling hard to focus his bleary eyes. "We are?"

"That's what you told me yesterday. You said, 'Sinner, let's go get some fine trout.' The sun's up. Here I am. Why don't you put that gun down and come inside for a cup of tea?"

"You know what your problem is, Sinner? You are nosy."

"I am not. I'm helpful."

"You are?" Old Judge looks at me suspiciously. "If you're so all-fired helpful, why don't you help me find out who stole Old Satan? I can't trust anyone. Sinner, you didn't take my gun, did you? I need that gun in case that slick varmint comes to take away those children."

What is Old Judge talking about? "I didn't steal Old Satan. It's probably in your cabin somewhere. Do you want me to look?"

I gently guide him through the open door. Three jugs of Taos Lightning are uncorked on the table. "Why don't you sleep awhile, Saint J.L.?" I throw two chunks of wood in the stove.

Old Judge sits wearily on his cot. "I don't want to sleep. I want to think. I need another drink for courage. Hand me that jug, will you?"

I give the jug a shake. "It's empty. Why don't you let me fix you some hot tea? That will make you feel better."

"I shot at the varmint once, but I missed. I need Old Satan because I know he's coming back to Hell's Gate. Then I'll blast him. Thinks he can take away those two young ones. Slavery was abolished. I fought in that war. I know. He can't take them like they're slaves."

"What are you talking about, Saint J.L.?" I pour water from a bucket into a kettle and add loose tea. I set the kettle on the stove to boil.

"I'm talking about how I'm going to stop Pug Ryan. But first I need another swig of Taos Lightning. For courage, mind you."

I try to piece together what Old Judge is saying. How could he have known that Pug Ryan was coming for us?

"Nothing left. Not a drop," Old Judge moans.

"I've got tea ready for you. Maybe I can find some bread to go with it," I tell him. On the table I find a stale loaf wrapped in a handkerchief. When I unwrap the bread, something falls on the floor. It's a piece of paper, the kind from Pheme's sketchbook. I look again. There are words in Pheme's handwriting.

Saint J.L.—
Pug Ryan is coming to take us away tomorrow. I'm to work in the mine. Hattie's to go to some hotel. Don't try to follow me. Look after Hattie. I'm going to find Pa. I will return anything I borrow.
Pheme

Old Judge tries to lift the mug of tea to his mouth. His hands are shaking so much, most of it spills. "Darned blast it! That tea's too hot! You trying to burn me or something? Why don't you leave me alone? An intolerable inconvenience. You know, that's what people are. I don't need anybody and nobody needs me. That's the way I like it. Give me a jug, will you?"

"I can't."

"Why?"

"I'm your friend. You've had enough, Saint J.L. The Taos Lightning is all gone. Drink some tea instead."

Old Judge looks at me angrily. "Why don't you go away? I know what you are. That other one, now she wasn't a pest like you." He sinks back into his lumpy mattress, eyes closed, boots still on his feet. "I can't remember what her name was. Maybe you know her. I liked her best. You know why?"

"No, why, Saint J.L.?" I ask, quietly gathering all the guns and pistols and sabers and knives I can find.

"I liked her the best because she never laughed at me or asked me embarrassing questions. Next time the freighter comes, you know what I'm going to do?"

"No, what'll you do, Saint J.L.?" I cover him with a quilt.

"I'm going to have him bring me a pretty silk handkerchief for her."

"That's a good idea. How about a green one?"

"Not for you. You're a pest. For the other one. The one with the angry hair."

I tiptoe across the room. At the doorway, I look at Old Judge sleeping peacefully. I know he meant to help us. He meant to protect us from Pug Ryan. Even though he failed, at least he tried. That was something.

I drag the guns outside and hide them in the tall grass near the footbridge. Then I dump into the river what's left in every jug I can find. While I use old rope to tie the cabin door shut from the outside, I spot Sinbad. He slinks out from under a bush, plainly distressed. "Old Judge will be all right," I tell the dog. "Just make sure he doesn't wander out and get into any more trouble."

There's no time to lose. Fast as I can, I run out of Old Judge's yard, east to Columbine Creek. Pheme has Old Satan and he's on his way up Rabbit Ears Pass to find Pa. And I'm going with him.

## FOURTEEN

The woods along Columbine Creek are gloomy and dark. I try not to look too closely into shadows, because I'm afraid I'll see eyes. I try not to think as I run. Just keep my legs moving, moving. I have to catch up with Pheme. Somehow, I just have to.

Finally, I slow to a breathless trot. Branches whip against my face. My arms are scratched and my legs ache. My stomach growls. If only I brought along something to eat! Even one of Cousin Tirzah's cold, hard biscuits would taste fine just now. Can't think about food. I have to keep moving.

As I climb the mountain toward Rabbit Ears Pass, the trees seem to shrink and shrivel. Up here, the wind leans hard against any living, upright thing. Gnarled limber pine branches point in the same direction. Are they trying to tell me which way Pheme went? I leap over a small stream of snow water and decide to stop a moment to splash my face.

A furry brown marmot pokes his head up between rocks and looks curiously at me.

"Hello. Have you seen my brother?" I ask.

The marmot whistles a shrill warning and disappears.

"Pheme! Pheme!" I shout. Only my echo answers.

Now I can see the pass. The path winds up the summit along patches of snow and rocky ridges. I have only to make it to the top and down the other side. Then I look for the North Fork. Isn't that what the stranger said? If I were a bird, my journey would be so easy. From up in the sky, I could see my brother. Maybe I could see Pa, too.

I walk and walk. Overhead, dark clouds billow, big as the mountains they weigh against. I hug my elbows. Cold wind blows through my long-sleeved muslin dress. I left so quickly, I forgot to bring along my shawl. A ptarmigan soars overhead, screaming. Is he warning me of snow or rain? I stop and listen.

Far away, I hear the rumble of thunder. Or is it gunfire? I scramble over the flinty rocks that break and crumble under my heels. It is dangerous to be so unprotected when lightning starts. I have to keep moving.

The trail zigzags. At the summit, I look down the other side of the mountain for some sign of Pheme. Nothing. I hurry down, leaping and sliding. Once inside the protection of the forest again, I sit on a log to rest. I must think. What if Pheme did not come this way at all? What if I can't find him?

Fat raindrops fall on the dusty path and trickle down my nose. A slender finger of lightning flickers. Thunder rumbles. "Pheme!" I shout. What if God smites me with lightning, just like he did to Andy Meyers whose marker's in the cemetery? I'll be a scorched and shriveled mound of ashes. Tired and discouraged, I lean against a lodgepole pine and close my eyes. What should I do?

The rain batters branches overhead, pocketa-pocketa-pocketa. I huddle where the trees are thickest, hoping for protection. The back of my dress sticks to my skin. I shiver. It might be warmer to keep moving. Reluctantly, I start again down the trail, which is hilly and slippery with a slick layer of pine needles.

I follow a ridge covered with new pines and slide down into a gully deep enough to hide me. Before I can scramble up the other side, I feel the ground shake. More thunder? I crouch, waiting. Instead, silence.

Suddenly, there is an ominous clatter over rocks. I freeze, listening, flattened against the ground. When I feel brave enough to raise my head, I see something so awful it takes my breath away.

Less than fifty yards distant, an enormous grizzly rises on his haunches, grunting and wheezing. He sniffs the air and stares in all directions with his small piggy eyes. I can't move, I am so scared. For some reason, the bear hasn't figured out where I am. Maybe he can't smell me yet because of the way the wind is blowing. But I can smell him. His sweet, doglike scent fills the air and makes my stomach turn.

The grizzly's fur is shaggy, dark brown, and tipped with silver. When he moves, it seems to ripple with power. He thumps to the ground on four paws again and snorts with his broad, dish-faced head close to the path. He ambles slowly, scratching the hump above his shoulders against a tree. Branches crack. Using giant black curved claws, he tears up a rotten log. Is he looking for ants?

My leg is falling asleep, I've been crouching so long. When I move, rocks tumble. Instantly, the bear stands, towering nine feet into the air. He gives a long-drawn, high-pitched musical sniff.

Panic. A hunter never runs from a bear, Old Judge once told me. A grizzly gallops as fast as a horse. How can I escape?

The grizzly spots me. His eyes are red, bloodshot. Quick as thought, the fur rises on his great wide neck. He chomps his huge jaws. The air rings with the sound of sharp, clacking teeth. The bear lets out a horrible growl. Without thinking, I leap to my feet. I don't know where I'm going. I don't care. A tree. Climb a tree. But do grizzlies climb trees, too? I can't remember anything Lord Calvert ever said about trees. All I know is that if this bear spares me, I promise never to be afraid of ghosts again the rest of my life, so help me God.

Every pine I pass is wrong. Too few limbs for climbing. Too skinny. I find a lodgepole with enough toeholds to let me shimmy to the top. Sharp branches scrape my arms and legs as I scramble as high as I can go. A new awful thought races through my head. What if the tree bends and breaks?

When I look down, the bear's disappeared. I can't see anything except pine needles and branches. I *did* see a bear, didn't I? Or was it just a ghost? I shiver. My heart beats wildly and my throat feels raw. Little by little, my breath returns to normal. I look around, trying to decide what to do.

Beyond my tree is a small clearing and a deadfall of logs.

From my high perch I can see a darker patch of ground that looks as if it might be a narrow gulch about ten feet wide. I can't tell how deep. Dead logs crisscross every which way. In my haste to escape the bear, I lost the trail. Which way did I come? How will I find my way back?

Just as I climb down, I hear heavy crashing and thrashing coming through the distant stand of jack pines on the other side of the gulch. The grizzly! I scramble back up the tree.

But the creature bursting through the thicket is not a bear. It's an enormous elk. The buck's huge antlers rip and snap branches as it staggers between the trees. When the elk paws the ground, I can see that its shoulder is red with blood. A blast of gunfire fills the air. The elk turns and charges back the way it came. What happened to the hunter?

A rifle gleams for an instant in the sunshine, but I can't make out who's aiming it. Another blast. There's more crashing in the trees, and a terrible bellow.

Then, silence.

I try to cry out, but nothing comes from my mouth. "Hello?" I say finally. "Who's there?"

No one answers. I wait, hoping someone will come out of the woods. Someone who will save me.

All kinds of terrible thoughts race through my head. Lord Calvert told me that a bull elk stands taller than a man at the shoulder and when wounded can be a fierce fighter. What if the hunter had been gored? Suddenly, the person I had hoped would save me may be the very person I'll have to save. It takes me a long time to climb out of the tree again.

"Hello! Hello? Anyone there?" I keep calling, moving cautiously toward the gulch. Now I can see that the narrow ditch is covered with a large fallen log. The log is the only way across. I peer between the trees, afraid to cross that log, afraid to see what might be on the other side.

I scream. For coming toward me, rocking from side to side in a strange unearthly manner, is the bloody bodiless head of the elk! Like some wandering evil spirit, the elk head shifts from side to side. Its long tongue wags. Its strange terrible eyes gaze upward, nowhere. Worse yet, the great head stumbles forward on human legs! What kind of monster is this?

Terrified, I dash back up the tree. This time I'm certain I really have seen a ghost. The ghost head of the bull elk. I peer down from the perch and watch the terrible head wobble to the fallen log to cross the gully. Closer, closer it comes. I cannot scream. I can't do anything except watch.

Suddenly, the head seems to lose its balance. It falls into the gulch. There's a crash and the sound of a human crying for help. How can that be?

The wind blows and my perch shifts. I gaze hard toward the thicket, toward the gully, but nothing emerges.

Even though my legs shake, I climb down. This is my chance to escape. I'll dash the other direction, away from that wandering elk head. But as I do, I hear something crashing heavily among the trees. I take one look toward the gulch. My brother, bloody and covered with dirt, scrambles into view!

"Pheme!" I cry in disbelief.

He staggers to his feet carrying Old Judge's huge gun, Old Satan. "Stay where y-y-y-you are!" he calls feebly, and gestures beyond the deadfall.

I turn, just in time to see the grizzly lumbering in our direction. His head's down. He smells the elk.

Without any urging from my brother, I shimmy back up the pine. But what about Pheme? I can hear the bear huff as he hurries closer, closer. The bear's enormous body splits branches and knocks apart logs as if they were only paper. The bear pauses, stands, and sniffs.

Pheme crouches behind a fallen tree with the gun resting on a log just the way Old Judge taught him. The bear has not spotted him yet. *Run, Pheme, run!* But Pheme doesn't move. Why doesn't he escape? Surely the bear would rather eat the elk than him. The gun barrel glints.

*What if you only wound the bear, Pheme? Forget your pride. Get out of there!*

I can hardly stand to watch. When I glimpse his face, it's bloody. What if he's been hurt? What if he doesn't have the strength to reload? That old gun isn't reliable, Old Judge admitted that to me. There's always the chance it will misfire. *Don't shoot! Run!*

The great bear drops to four legs and pokes a rotten log with his long, sharp claws. He's still unaware of Pheme's presence. I hold my breath as he moves closer to Pheme's hiding place. Twenty yards, fifteen yards, ten yards. The longer I watch, the more enormous the bear seems to become.

The gun roars. The bear turns and spots Pheme. The gun blasts again. A red gash rips across the bear's shoulder. As the bear lunges toward Pheme, his forelegs swing forward as if in slow motion. The gun blazes again.

Then silence. Smoke fills the air. I can see nothing.

"Pheme?" I cry. Somehow I'm on the ground. I'm

scrambling toward the gulch, terrified. "Pheme!" I slump against a tree, unable to breathe. He's dead. I'm sure he's dead. I cover my face with my hands and sob.

"Hattie! Stop crying and help me!"

"Pheme!" I shout joyfully, and plunge through the trees. A huge shape lies sprawled on the ground. Carefully, I come closer, closer. The dead bear is bigger than I imagined. My brother's legs are caught beneath the giant fallen creature. He is trapped but he is alive!

"Do you think anything's broken?" I ask.

"Can't tell."

Straining every muscle, I dig my heels into the ground and pull. Pheme's blood-covered hands are slick as peeled onion. My feet slip in the mud and pine needles, and I fall. I stand and try again. Slowly, I can feel him pulling free, wriggling out from under the enormous pile of muscle and fur. He crawls on all fours away from the bear and slowly staggers to a clearing.

"Can you walk? You're bleeding, Pheme."

"I'm all right. The b-b-b-blood's mostly the bear's." Pheme wipes his hands on his shirt and fumbles for his gun. He peers into the gully.

I join him. The antlers are as big as two huge branches of an enormous tree. "You want to take *those*?" I ask in disbelief. How can he be thinking about his trophy at a time like this?

He shrugs. "They're t-t-t-oo heavy."

I fold my arms in front of myself and stare hard at him. "You were going after Pa without me. Why'd you leave me? It wasn't fair. He's my pa, too."

"I didn't f-f-find him. Not a trace."

"Pa's probably on the other side of some other mountain. Don't worry, Pheme. We'll find him."

Pheme shrugs. A cold night's on its way and we have no food, no extra warm clothes. My brother's scraped up pretty bad and the side of my face throbs from my tumble out of the tree. I know we have to go back, even though I don't want to. "Can't we keep looking?" I beg.

Pheme shakes his head. Our search for Pa has ended, at least for today.

"I'll go back to Cousin Tirzah's, but only on one condition. You have to promise me you won't run away again without me."

Pheme sighs. "I promise."

"What about the grizzly and the buck? Nobody will believe you shot anything so big by yourself."

"You want to c-c-c-carry them?" Pheme starts out through the moonlit woods to the trail, Old Satan over his shoulder.

"Pheme!" I shout. "When you called to me, when you were trapped under the bear, did you notice? Did you notice something different about the way you talked?"

My brother stops and looks at me in puzzlement.

"You didn't stutter. Not once. Pheme, why do you think that was?"

"Guess I was too s-s-scared," he replies, and grins at his own joke. We both laugh. But I know the truth. Pheme is the bravest person this side of the Continental Divide.

## FIFTEEN

Cousin Tirzah acts real happy to see us again. And why shouldn't she? If Pheme and I never returned, she wouldn't have anything to hand over to Mr. Pug Ryan. "Whatsoever you ask, it shall be; do we ask in faith, believing. Amen," she says solemnly to me.

"I have to tell Lord Calvert about Pheme's bear and his elk antlers," I reply, hurrying outside so I don't have to listen to Cousin Tirzah preach or say anything about Pug Ryan coming back. I spot Lord Calvert and Samuel and tell them about the grizzly and the buck. "Each antler's four feet long, almost as tall as me. I counted twelve points, six on each side. My brother shot the elk, cut off the head with his hunting knife and then—"

"Delightful story, my dear," Lord Calvert interrupts. "You certainly have a nasty scrape on your face." Samuel is loading supplies on the pack mule for another hunt. Lord Calvert is in such a hurry this morning, he hasn't even eaten breakfast. "Where did you say your brother shot this bear and elk?"

"Up past Rabbit Ears Pass, on the way to Hitchens Gulch. I guess that bear must have been nine feet tall," I say, hoping that he's really interested, that he's not just trying to be polite. I draw a map with a stick in the dirt outside the cabin. I pace the ground to show how big that grizzly really was. I stretch my arms to show how wide that span of antlers stretched.

"Harriet, stop plaguing Lord Calvert with your lies. You have a wicked, wild imagination!" Cousin Tirzah scolds from the cabin doorway.

Just as Lord Calvert is about to leave, Pheme hurries to him and boldly says, "If you like, I can show y-y-y-you where I shot the b-b-bear and elk."

Lord Calvert looks at Pheme with one eyebrow raised. He glances at Samuel and then at scowling Cousin Tirzah.

"The boy is idiotic, your lordship," Cousin Tirzah says, her hands on her hips. "And he's probably lying."

"I spotted tracks last week larger than I have ever seen before. I want that grizzly," Lord Calvert says. "Madam, describe what you saw when this young man returned last night."

"If you're asking if he was carrying a bearskin, no. He was not, sir," Cousin Tirzah replies. "All he had was a poor excuse for a gun. Told me he borrowed it from Old Judge."

"Did you notice anything else about his clothing?" Lord Calvert asks.

"He was dirty, same as always. Now that I think of it, he was a bloody mess, as if he's been cleaning a whole bushel of fish. The blood might have come from a raccoon or a deer. I tell you, the boy's idiotic. He could never shoot a grizzly," Cousin Tirzah insists.

Lord Calvert pauses. He looks directly at Pheme. "Are you telling me the truth about this nine-foot-tall bear? I insist on the truth."

Pheme nods determinedly.

"All right," Lord Calvert announces. "Samuel, saddle two more horses. We're taking this boy with us to show us the place where he slew the great grizzly."

Pheme looks thrilled. He hurries to get Old Judge's gun. Cousin Tirzah shakes her head but does not try to stop him. "Fools," she mutters under her breath as Pheme, Lord Calvert, and Samuel disappear between the trees.

All day I listen between chores for the sound of harness and hooves. What is taking Pheme so long? At one point, I nearly sneak away to check on Old Judge. I resist the temptation. After all, he needs a full day or two to sleep off the effects of his drinking spree. Willie and I wander down to the lake and throw rocks in the water.

Suddenly, we hear shouting and barking. I grab Willie and hurry back to Cousin Tirzah's cabins. Into the clearing Lord Calvert leads the two packhorses, heavily loaded with the enormous skin of a bear. A grizzly's head nods up and down on the horse's rump. Four huge paws with claws stick out of a rolled canvas tarp strapped to another horse. On the third horse wobble Pheme's enormous elk antlers—my ghost. I can hardly wait to invite Old Judge to see Pheme's prize for himself.

"Will you look at that!" Eddie exclaims.

Leading the packhorses on foot are Samuel and Pheme. Pheme smiles broadly. Lord Calvert dismounts and sweeps the ground in front of Cousin Tirzah with his hat. He snaps his fingers and commands Samuel to begin unloading. "How do you like my grizzly and elk antlers? Both are fine specimens. Took the three of us nearly four hours to skin the bear. Unfortunately a mountain lion took most of the elk. But the antlers are intact and impressive. They'll look handsome over my fireplace at my country estate."

"*Your* grizzly? *Your* elk?" I protest. "That bear and those antlers belong to my brother! He's the one who shot them. Isn't that right, Pheme?"

"They *did* belong to your brother," Lord Calvert replies. "Except he sold them. Show her."

Pheme holds up a large money pouch. He shakes the coins inside for everyone to hear.

"I could not return to London without my prize, the great silvertip bear, the Monarch of the Mountain. Whatever would my friends say? Now I can go home with my head held high. No one need know I was not the one who brought this vicious creature down."

Since Pheme does not look disappointed, neither am I. But before I can take a closer look at the glittering coins, I hear the sound of jangling harness. Somebody's coming.

Mr. Pug Ryan arrives in a cloud of dust, his two-wheeled carriage pulled by a white horse. I am unable to say or do anything as Cousin Tirzah tosses him our carpetbag. She turns to Pheme and says coolly, "Lord Calvert is a man of his word. And I am a woman of my word, too. Hand over the money, boy. It's only fair. It's what you and your sister owe me for your keep."

Pheme's eyes widen with shock and disbelief.

"Well, isn't this wonderful?" Lord Calvert says cheerfully. "I get my bear and elk. You, madam, are finally paid for all your troubles. And these children find honest employment. See how well everything has worked out?"

Everything has not worked out well at all. I watch, horrified, as Pheme pitches the money pouch to the ground near Cousin Tirzah's feet. She picks it up and smiles grimly. "Praise be the Lord. Now hand over the gun, too. Someone is going to have to return it to Old Judge as soon as he's sober. They're all yours, Mr. Ryan," Cousin Tirzah says.

"Right this way and I'll take you to the Coming Wonder and the Grand Imperial Hotel," Pug Ryan says, and motions to me and Pheme. "Come along and don't give me any trouble," he warns in a low voice. Cousin Tirzah gives us a push. Pug Ryan leans out of the carriage and pulls me up by my arm.

"Hattie!" Willie shouts, his face streaked with tears. "Don't go, Hattie!"

Eddie, Patience, and Minnie cower like frightened rabbits. Their eyes dart from me to Pheme to their mother and back again. They don't say anything.

I wave halfheartedly. Under my breath, I whisper, "Pheme, make a run for it!"

But Pheme won't run. He refuses to leave me and climbs slowly into the carriage.

"That's the ticket, boy," Pug Ryan hisses. "If you ever want to see your sister again, do as I say." He raises the whip over the horse's head.

Gunfire explodes. The horse rears and prances. Pug Ryan reins in the frightened creature. "What the devil—"

"My thoughts exactly!" a voice booms.

I twist in my seat. In complete amazement I watch Old

Judge coming through the trees. He's got one of his big guns pressed against his shoulder, aimed straight at Pug Ryan's head.

"Now, now!" Pug Ryan protests. Beads of sweat pop on his forehead. "This ain't any of your business, Judge."

I glance at Cousin Tirzah. Her face is pale and she's biting her lip. Any moment Pug Ryan is about to be blown to bits. "I'll call the sheriff!" she says shrilly. "You put that gun down and let Mr. Ryan be on his way."

"Never," says Old Judge, and spits on the ground. "You let those children go, Ryan."

"Why should we be afraid of you? Mr. Ryan can give the children up today, but he can always come back another time when you're not here to protect them," Cousin Tirzah says, as if her old fierce courage has suddenly returned. "Besides, everybody knows you can't see to shoot anymore, Judge."

Old Judge squeezes the trigger. The gun fires, Pug Ryan's soft brown fedora flies from his head and lands in the dust.

Pug Ryan gasps. His collar's stained with sweat. His hands are shaking. I glance at Lord Calvert out of the corner of my eye. His expression is pale. His lips twitch.

" 'You tread upon my patience,' " Old Judge says. "If it's money you need to stake yourself in a new claim, Ryan, there's plenty in the bag Tirzah's holding. Isn't that right, Mr. Lord?"

Lord Calvert nods eagerly.

"I'm sure you'd rather have your cash in one lump sum and not have to wait for these children's wages to come into your pocket, now wouldn't you, Ryan?" Old Judge says.

Pug Ryan licks his lips. His eyes dart beseechingly toward Tirzah. "Come on," he says. "Give me the money."

"Not yet," Old Judge shouts.

Pug Ryan freezes.

"First, let Hattie and Pheme climb down," Old Judge orders. Pheme nudges me with his elbow and I climb with him to the ground. We hurry behind Old Judge, who hasn't once lowered his gun.

Cousin Tirzah picks up the money bag and shakes it tenderly as if it contains all that is precious. I hold my breath. What if she refuses to give it up? To my surprise, in one large arc she swings the bag to Ryan in a gesture of—what? I don't know.

As soon as that bag clinks and crashes inside the carriage at his feet, Pug Ryan cracks the whip. The horse races away in a choking cloud of dust. Lord Calvert and Samuel scurry to the safety of their cabin. Cousin Tirzah collapses on an overturned barrel. Old Judge finally lowers his gun.

"Saint J.L., how'd you get out of your cabin?" I ask. "How'd you find your guns?"

Old Judge smiles. "The window, Sinner. And Sinbad helped me find the guns."

"You think Mr. Ryan will come back for us?" I ask quietly.

Old Judge scratches the back of his head. "I suspect he's headed out of town at this very moment. Probably on his way to some other mining camp. He won't be seen here again. Too much bum debt. Besides, he's got the only thing he wanted—gold. Tirzah knows that, too."

I glance at Cousin Tirzah. Her children have wandered

away from her. Her head is lowered and her face is covered by her strong hands.

Pheme picks up Pug Ryan's hat and sticks his finger through the hole. "Good shot." He smiles at Old Judge and hands him Old Satan.

"Only had two bullets. Guess the second one was lucky," Old Judge says, and winks. " 'There's a divinity that shapes our ends, / Rough-hew them how we will.' *Hamlet,* Act Five, Scene Two. Am I right this time, Boss?"

Pheme nods and grins.

## SIXTEEN

The season is changing. Aspen tree leaves, once green, spangle the mountainsides and meadows with bright yellow and gold. Some mornings the air smells of snow. Nearby peaks are dusted white. Winter's coming.

Cousin Tirzah never mentions the day Old Judge rescued us from Pug Ryan. I don't bring up the subject and neither does Pheme. We figure Cousin Tirzah's decided to do her duty by us and we'd just as soon not give her cause to think twice.

Three weeks ago Lord Calvert and Samuel left. Since then, five other hunters have been boarding in the guest cabin. We don't know how long they'll be staying or if there will be any more until spring. There's a new bachelor in town; his name is Picnic Jim. You ask him how he is and he always has the same answer: "Having a picnic." I suppose that's how he got his name. Whenever he brings his laundry for Cousin Tirzah, he stays awhile to jaw. Once or twice I've even seen her smile at his jokes.

Last night I heard a screech owl again. It sounded like a woman paining. It's a sign a bad winter's coming, Old Judge says. Ever since his spree, he's been the same kind old gentleman and friend. He promised me he's cured of liquoring forever. I believe him.

I admit I'm making a real effort to be more helpful to Cousin Tirzah these days. Soon as she says there's laundry to be hung, I get right to work. Pheme goes out of his way to snare extra rabbits or catch extra fish. Cousin Tirzah doesn't complain about us anymore, but I know we're burdensome. Late one night I wake up and catch her adding columns of ledger-book figures by the light of a candle.

"Go to sleep, girl," she tells me when she sees me watching her. It is the way she speaks—not the words—that surprises me. Her voice doesn't have the hard edge I'm used to. She speaks soft, almost tender.

I close my eyes.

I still miss Pa. Every week I go into town and check for a letter. We haven't had one yet. I keep hoping.

One day, after Willie and I have gone to the cemetery to do a little decorating with wildflowers and sparkling red quartz, we notice a gaunt shape coming down the road into Last Chance. Another hard-luck miner probably. He leads a burro with ribs that poke out sharp as elbows.

I decide to stop and watch the stranger pass. Maybe I'll ask him if he's been up Neversummer Range. Before I can speak, I notice something peculiar. It's the way the skinny, dusty man with the beard walks. The toe of his right foot goes out flippity-flop to the south, while the left steers straight ahead. Only one other person I know walks like that.

"Pa!" I yell. I grab Willie and run. The man with the bony burro pushes back his hat from his forehead. His blue eyes go all shiny.

"That you, Hattie?" Pa says, opening his arms. "Well, hello to you, gal!"

I give Pa an enormous hug. He looks at my face carefully. "What happened? Where did you get that scar?"

"Grizzly," I say.

Pa smiles like he knows I'm fibbing. "I mean, I fell out of a tree after a grizzly got done chasing me."

"Ho-ho! I see! Sounds as if you've been busy while I've been away." Pa's Adam's apple bounces on his thin neck when he laughs. "And how's your brother?"

"Fine," I say, deciding to let Pheme tell the bear story. "Pa, are you all right? You look like you haven't eaten in months. Did you get my letters? Why didn't you write? We were so worried. Now that you're back, we're not orphans anymore, are we, Pa?"

"Hold on there, gal. I can't keep up with you. I got your letters. That's why I sent word with that prospector. I would have sent a real letter except I didn't have any money. But what's this about being orphans? You aren't orphans as long as you have me."

"You sure, Pa?"

"I swear it."

"On a stack of Bibles?"

"On a stack of Bibles."

I sigh and give Pa's rough hand a squeeze. "I bet you're hungry. I'll fix you something to eat."

"Didn't find enough gold up there to fill a hen's tooth, I'm afraid. Bad luck, I guess. Just plain bad luck," Pa murmurs.

"It's all right, Pa," I reply, cheerful as I can. He looks so sad, like the life went out of him up there prospecting all alone. "We just wanted you to come home safe so we could be together again. That's what me and Pheme really wanted. We don't need the gold. Something's sure to turn up. It always does. Isn't that what you always say?"

"Guess I do," he admits, and walks hand-in-hand into the clearing near Cousin Tirzah's cabins with Willie and me. The burro follows us. "Where is your brother?" Pa asks.

"He's hunting with Old Judge again. A month ago he shot an elk and a grizzly, just like a grown man. Old Judge taught Pheme how to use a gun. You'll like Old Judge," I say. Pa looks tired and confused.

"Hungry!" Willie shouts. There's smoke coming from the chimney, and it smells like venison and onions.

Cousin Tirzah greets us from the doorway, smoothes her apron, and flashes a nervous smile. "Good to see you again, Cousin James. We weren't sure you'd be coming back—so soon." Her eyes dart this way and that, examining Pa's prospecting outfit.

"Not much to show for myself, ma'am," Pa replies wearily.

"You got *any* gold dust?"

"Not enough to fill five fingernails." Pa reaches in his pocket and pulls out a dirty handkerchief with the ends tied together. He places the bundle carefully on the ground and begins to undo the knots. "I did have the good luck to meet a fellow from Illinois. He had better diggings than me. Only problem was, he caught pneumonia up there in the cold and damp. I nursed him back to health best I could. Well, this fellow was so grateful, seeing as how he was left alone in the whole world and ready to die, he lent me some of his gold dust. He and I are going into the dry-goods business together in Galena, Illinois. With this gold I should be able to buy a wagon and team to take myself and the children." He sighs and looks at the mountains. "Twelve hundred miles back to Illinois."

"How much you got?" Cousin Tirzah asks, squinting. She wipes her hands on her apron and leans over to inspect the small mound of precious yellowish powder. She pinches it, sniffs it, holds it in the palm of her hand. Then she carefully replaces each crumb in Pa's handkerchief. "You ain't got much. And seeing as how the price of a team and wagon is dear now that everybody and his brother are trying to get out of the mountains before snow closes the pass, I'd say you're going to have to do some clever bargaining to get what you need to make it to Illinois. Don't forget you got to buy supplies. Don't forget you and your children got to eat."

Pa holds up one hand as if to stop Cousin Tirzah from saying anything more. "Cousin Tirzah," he says, trying to charm a smile out of her, "you fed and housed my children, and I'm grateful. Name your price."

I hold my breath, waiting for Cousin Tirzah to announce how much Pa owes her. I wait to hear her say what's her fair share of that borrowed gold—all the money Pa has in the world to get us back to Illinois. But she never mentions the sums from her ledger book. "You don't owe me nothing, Cousin James. I'm not going to take what little you got. The good Lord provides, but I don't want the burden of feeling guilty I had a hand in preventing you from getting across the Plains in one piece. Pay me when you can, Cousin James. Until then, we'll just call things square between us."

Right then I decide not to mention Pug Ryan, the Coming Wonder, or the Grand Imperial Hotel. What's done is done.

"Come inside and have some vittles," Cousin Tirzah says.

"I would be much obliged, thank you," Pa replies. He removes his battered felt hat and steps inside.

Cousin Tirzah generously heaps a plate with venison and boiled potatoes. She places it in front of Pa and leaves the room. He eats through one plate and two more refills I spoon up for him. All the while, I sit and watch him chew. He seems more familiar to me when he's eating.

"You going to shave that beard off?" I ask.

Pa stops eating for a moment and smiles at me. "Don't you like it?"

"No. Can't see your face. I liked you better the way you were before."

Pa sops up the last of the gravy with a biscuit and pops it in his mouth. The food seems to revive him. "Hattie, we'll be leaving soon as we can. What do you think about that?"

"That's fine, Pa," I say slowly. I can't quite believe it's true. We're going back to Illinois.

Pa takes his pipe out of his pocket.

"Need some tobacco, Pa?" I whisper.

"I'm afraid I do. Forgot I ran out months ago. The dinner was so good, I just naturally reached for a smoke."

"I'll get you some." I pad quietly across the room and

open a tin I discovered behind a fireplace stone. It's the late Mr. Throckmorton's tobacco. I don't think he'll mind. "Here you go."

Pa nods and smiles. "I see you've found your way around Cousin Tirzah's home rather nicely."

I nod. "Cousin Tirzah's not so bad once you understand her."

Sinbad barks. I run outside just as Pheme and Old Judge tie the burro to a tree. Slung over the burro is a fine deer. "Pheme, Pa's come back!" I call. "Come see!"

Pa steps cautiously from the cabin into the yard. What will Pheme do?

My brother doesn't hesitate. He runs to Pa and embraces him. Now I can see how tall my brother's grown—nearly past Pa's shoulder. Pheme awkwardly wipes something from his eyes. I know Pheme is trying to be manly and all grown up, but he's crying.

"Pa, this is our friend, Old Judge, also called Saint J.L.," I say.

"Also called Joseph Wescott. How do you do, sir?" Old Judge extends his hand to shake Pa's hand. "You have fine children, fine children."

Pa nods and rests his trembling hands on both our shoulders. I feel as if I'm looking at Old Judge for the first time. I realize I've never seen him in the company of so many people before. Old Judge appears highly uncomfortable.

"You've taught Pheme well. There's enough venison there for a feast," Pa says.

"Tomorrow, we'll have a proper celebration," Cousin Tirzah says, beaming. "Rainbow trout, larded biscuits full weight, and yellow beans boiled forty-eight hours. You'll come too, won't you, Old Judge?"

"No, ma'am. Thank you, ma'am, but no," Old Judge replies quietly. "Must get home now." Without looking back as he enters the trees, he raises one hand and gives us a short wave. At that moment, I realize that Pheme and I will soon be leaving Old Judge. And we may never see him again.

## SEVENTEEN

For two days we've been packing supplies for our trip back to Illinois. Pa bought a secondhand buckboard and a team of horses. There's not much time left before the pass closes with drifting snow. We have to hurry.

When the moment finally comes to say good-bye, Pheme and I go to Old Judge's cabin. Cold wind from Lone Squaw sounds sad and lonesome through the trees. Sinbad greets us, wagging his tail joyfully. Old Judge is sitting in front of his fireplace, mending a snowshoe. He does not look up because he knows it is us by the special way we knock.

"You're leaving, then?" Old Judge asks. "Well, best of luck to you." He stands and shakes my brother's hand like Pheme was a grown-up. "Boss, remember all you learned. Value yourself and face the world with a bright blade of honor, courage, and determination. I'd like you to have Old Satan. You've earned him and I know you'll treat him well."

Old Judge holds out the gleaming gun that saved Pheme's life. Maybe mine, too.

My brother takes Old Satan in his fine, pale hands. He nods, blinking hard.

"These I made for you, Sinner," Old Judge says. "Your own Norwegian snowshoes. You'll be the only girl in Illinois with a pair made from Lone Squaw willow."

"They're beautiful, Saint J.L.!" My voice quavers strangely. "I'll write to you if you'll write to me. Galena doesn't sound like such a bad place to send a letter. Pa and his new partner are going to run a dry-goods store. He said I can help him after school. Maybe I'll send you and Sinbad some licorice or peppermints. You'd like that, wouldn't you?"

"Sure, Sinner, anything you do's all right with me." Old Judge laughs and tousles my angry hair.

Pa's whistle can be heard clear to this side of the lake. He's calling us to come. It's almost time to start our trip home.

"I almost forgot," Old Judge says quickly. "I have one more surprise for you, Sinner. It came with the last shipment the freighter brought." From above the fireplace he bashfully hands me a small square shape wrapped in tissue.

I tear away the paper and discover a delicate green silk handkerchief. Pressing the softness to my face, I whisper, "It's so beautiful!"

"You can use it next time you feel like having a good, long cry," Old Judge says. He grins. But when I look closely, I notice that he's the one with the misty eyes.

"Saint J.L., I won't forget you," I promise. I tuck the silk handkerchief in my pocket. I give Old Judge a hug and rush out the door with my snowshoes. There is a big lump in my throat and the path is suddenly so bleary, I can hardly see where I'm going.

Pheme and I don't say anything as we hurry across the footbridge back to Cousin Tirzah's for the last time. Pa packs my snowshoes in the wagon, but Pheme insists on carrying his gun.

"Good-bye, Willie!" I say, planting a kiss on his confused, dear little face. "Good-bye, Eddie! Good-bye, Minnie! Good-bye, Patience! Good-bye, Cousin Tirzah!"

"Good-bye and God bless you both!" Cousin Tirzah says, and gives each of us an awkward embrace. Even Eddie, Patience, and Minnie seem sad to see us go.

Pheme and I climb in the wagon and let our feet dangle out the end. "Giddyap!" Pa shouts. The horses strain and pull. I wave good-bye one last time, holding overhead my new silk handkerchief. The bright green floats and flutters in the wind like Mama's favorite melody, "Sweet Hour of Prayer." The road to Berthoud Pass curves. Lone Squaw Lake disappears.

"Pheme," I ask as we bump along, "what if one day when I'm old, maybe fifteen or sixteen, I forget Old Judge? Do you think I won't be able to remember what he looks like?"

"Nope," Pheme replies. He reaches inside our carpetbag for his sketchbook. Sure enough, there's page after page of pencil drawings. Old Judge fishing. Old Judge playing checkers. Old Judge shooting at targets. And there are funny sketches, too: Old Judge on his hands and knees, his nose nearly to the ground, saying, "Come back here, hopper!" Old Judge flying over the head of the burro he called his

Rocky Mountain canary, the time he tried to make the noisy critter ford the creek.

I laugh and laugh till I'm crying, and so is Pheme. Maybe someday we'll come back to Lone Squaw Lake. Until then, I have my brother's drawings. And something more. I know now that the thing about loving is that I never have to stop, even when that person is gone far away. I can still keep Old Judge in my heart, the same way I keep Mama.

# About the Author

Trained as a journalist, Laurie Lawlor worked for many years as a freelance writer and editor before devoting herself full-time to the creation of children's books. She enjoys many speaking engagements at schools and libraries, and her books have been nominated for many awards. She lives in Evanston, Illinois, with her husband, son, daughter, and two large Labrador retrievers. Her books include the *Addie Across the Prairie* series, the *Heartland* series, *How to Survive Third Grade*, *The Worm Club*, *Gold in the Hills*, and *Little Women* (a movie novelization). Her nonfiction work, *Shadow Catcher: The Life and Work of Edward S. Curtis*, won the Carl Sandburg Award for nonfiction (1995) and the Golden Kite Honor Book Award (1995).

**NEW YORK MILLS
PUBLIC LIBRARY**
401 Main Street
New York Mills, N.Y. 13417
(315)736-5391

MEMBER
MID-YORK LIBRARY SYSTEM
Utica, N.Y. 13502

**120100**